AF241676

OUTFOXED

ON THE RANCH, BOOK 4

JODI PAYNE

BA TORTUGA

This is a work of fiction. Names, characters, places, and incidents either are the product of the author's imagination or are used fictitiously. Any resemblance to actual events, locales, organizations, or persons, living or dead, is entirely coincidental and beyond the intent of either the author or the publisher.

Outfoxed
Copyright © 2025 by Jodi Payne & BA Tortuga

Edited by LC Hinson

Cover illustration by AJ Corza
http://www.seeingstatic.com/
Cover content is for illustrative purposes only and any person depicted on the cover is a model.

ISBN: 978-1-963644-12-8

All rights reserved. This book is licensed to the original purchaser only. Duplication or distribution via any means is illegal and a violation of international copyright law, subject to criminal prosecution and upon conviction, fines, and/or imprisonment. No part of this book may be reproduced or transmitted in any form or by any means, electronic or mechanical, including photocopying, recording, or by any information storage and retrieval system, without the written permission of the Publisher, except where permitted by law. To request permission and all other inquiries, contact Tygerseye Publishing, LLC, www.tygerseyepublishing.com

Published by Tygerseye Publishing, LLC
April, 2025
Printed in the USA

OUTFOXED

JODI PAYNE & BA TORTUGA

Outfoxed is an opposites attract, hurt/comfort, found family romance featuring an injured bull rider at the end of his career and a widower single dad derailed by a mental health crisis.

Bull rider Trent James might be a little broken. He's a cowboy recovering from a terrible wreck, going through the grind of surgeries and physical therapy and trying not to have a meltdown. Thank goodness for his friends and neighbors Rope and Jude, who keep him up and moving and getting better.

Callum Fox is broken for a totally different reason. When he heads to Texas to visit his friends, he's looking to get away from too many hours as a CEO and too many memories of his late husband. He wants to spend more time with his daughter, and he needs to figure out what he's going to do with the rest of his life.

The two of them come together and find kindred spirits in each other. But sometimes it's tough to glue the broken parts back together, and they have to find out where they fit and what they can do to support each other, even when the storm gets bad. Can Fox and Trent make a life together, or will they be unable to mend their shattered pieces?

THE ON THE RANCH SERIES

Tending Tyler

Roped In

Diamonds in the Rough

Outfoxed

These are all stand-alone novels
and can be read in any order.

As always, to our wives.

1

"Trent, buddy. You gotta get your shit together. You gotta wake up, because you're worrying folks."

Trent tilted his head, or he tried to. *Okay, that hurt. Let's not do that again. All right?*

All right, he told himself. What was the very last thing he remembered?

He was in... somewhere. Nashville? He thought it was Nashville.

Maybe New Orleans? Could be New Haven. Somewhere with an N.

Surely not New Mexico? Hmm.

No, it was definitely Nashville. The sidewalks singing— he remembered that.

Okay, good. And then after that?

He took a deep breath. Oh, yeah, that hurt too.

So, he must have been riding. Hurting like this meant a wreck.

He couldn't smell dirt, so that was probably good.

Of course, if he couldn't smell dirt, he didn't know where he was, and he had to wake up?

That meant he was either in the hospital or in an ambulance. Both of those were bad.

Didn't sound like an ambulance. Didn't feel like one either. They tended to be tight and loud and jostly, and someone was always bugging you.

"I'm serious, Trent. You wake your happy ass up. I will kick your butt."

Okay, that voice—he knew that was Rope. His best buddy. His traveling partner. His neighbor. If Rope was here, it was serious.

He licked his lips, wondering if he should ask for a drink or what the hell had happened to him first.

"Thirsty," was the word he croaked out.

Well. That was fair. His body decided what it wanted to do, and fuck his curious brain.

"Yeah? How about some ice chips? They don't want you puking."

"Surgery?" he asked, because that was the answer to no puking.

"You know it, buddy. You got yourself all tore up. Shoulder. Collarbone. Your right arm. Got some good bruises too. But they pretty much had to put that whole right side back together. It's gross. Silas will be over the moon to see."

"Ice chips."

So, the shoulder blade and the collarbone break explained why it hurt to nod. At least his mouth wasn't wired shut. That always sucked.

"Did I win any money?"

A sliver of ice slid over his lips, and he moaned. Oh, that felt so good. So damn good.

"No, sir. Not a dime. Gonna make some money off talking about this wreck, if you're lucky."

He should have retired last year.

"Home." If Trent was broke, he needed to be home.

"Day after tomorrow. I rented a van. We'll just drive it."

"Jude?"

Rope snorted. "We got a baby coming, man. Any day. He's at home. Just in case."

"The boy?"

"I am not bringing my son out here to drive. He's not old enough to help with that part. No, he is in school. You gotta focus, man. It's April. He's in school."

"Right. Sorry." He wasn't going to say that he didn't need Rope to drive him home, or that he was going to manage it by himself or any of that shit because they knew each other well enough to know better. He'd driven Rope more places than he cared to admit, and his buddy had done the same for him. That was what traveling partners were for.

Not that Rope was riding. Rope was retired. Rope had been retired for something like... two years, right?

They hadn't gone backward in time, surely.

No. Rope said there was a baby coming, and they'd just done that, seemed like. Back last summer? Maybe they started back in the spring, after talking to every damn human being in Texas about having a baby.

The simple fact was that Rope was still retired.

"Man. I'm here for the sponsors. I was doing a signing and introducing that new bull."

This was why a man had a riding partner.

Because they knew each other, and they didn't have to ask stupid questions.

Rope would just give him stupid answers. That was how it ought to be.

"Did we go in on yaks together?"

Rope cracked up, the laughter covering up the constant

beeping. "You fucking know we did. You know how much yak butter sells for? You know how funny it is to watch cowboys try to milk a yak?"

"Want to go home."

"I know. When you get the tubes out of your arms and out of your dick, we're on it. We'll just drive home, and get you settled."

"Swear to God?"

"I swear by all I hold holy, man, and I got a lot of that." Rope chuckled and leaned down, kissed his forehead like he was a little boy. "It's time to hang your bull rope up, man, and come home. We'll raise yaks and horses and cows and be happy."

Rope was right. He hated to admit it, but he might have done ridden his last ride.

Maybe it was time to become an old cowboy with the ranch.

2

F ox sat at the kitchen table with a half-empty bottle of beer in one hand and his cell phone in the other.

He'd told himself he'd make this call as soon as Amelia was in bed, but she'd been asleep for an hour, and he was still working up the nerve. He'd finished one beer, started another, and was fidgeting with his stupid phone instead of dialing Jude.

"Make the call, Fox. It's just a phone call. It's just a friend. Make the stupid fucking call."

If anyone in the world was going to understand, it would be Jude. They'd met in a support group for single dads who'd lost their spouses years ago, and by the time Jude moved to Texas, they'd learned a lot about each other. A lot of personal things. Hard things. Jude had heard it all.

With all that history between them, he didn't know why it was so difficult to reach out now. Maybe it was because Jude was remarried and happy, and he was struggling?

But if he couldn't ask Jude, he couldn't ask anybody.

He put the phone down on the table and blinked at it

another second, then swiped the screen open and tapped Jude's name.

There.

It was ringing.

It wasn't until Jude answered that he realized what time it was.

"Hey, Fox. Long time. Everything okay?"

Right. People with kids didn't call each other after nine o'clock, so of course Jude would think there was something wrong.

And Jude was right, but that wasn't how he wanted to start this conversation.

"Hey, man. Yeah. Everything is fine. You know how it is, hard to find time to make a phone call these days."

"Oh, sure. I bet. Busy, busy. Mr. CEO."

"Yep. Busy." He was bad liar. He'd left his job over a week ago.

He'd stayed longer than he should have.

"Hang on, the new baby is sleeping."

"Oh, shit. I'm sorry. We can talk later, not big deal." He should have known better.

"No, no. It's okay. I'm out on the porch now, it's all good. So... how've you been?" Jude's question seemed to be addressing more than his health.

"Good, good." He rolled his eyes at himself. *You better start telling the truth, you idiot.* He took a sip of his beer. "Well, mostly. I've uh—well, things are—it's been a tough... couple of weeks."

A *year.* It had been a tough fucking year.

"Oh." Jude's tone changed and he hated the sound of sympathy, even if he needed a little of it. "Hey, I'm sorry to hear that. Is it Amelia?"

"Oh, no. No, she's fine. She's great." *She's just way too*

smart for me to pretend I'm okay anymore. "It's work, mostly, and... just me."

"Okay, I'm listening. What's going on? What can I do?"

He shrugged as if Jude could see him. "I don't know, man. I need, uh—my therapist says I should get some downtime, preferably out of the city, you know? And I was thinking—"

"You want to visit? Absolutely." Jude didn't hesitate, and that felt pretty good.

"Well, I didn't think about the new baby when I decided to call." That might be awkward.

"It's a big place, Fox. We have guest rooms. Did you want to come now? Or—?"

"No, Amelia has school. Soon though?"

"Right. You should come when school lets out. Bring Amelia and enjoy the air."

He took a deep breath through his nose and let it out slowly through his mouth as he'd been taught, feeling some of the anxiety loosen up in his chest. "Would that be okay? I really have to get away from here."

"Fox." He remembered that tone. "Come visit. Relax. We have acres of land, miles of sky, and enough clean air to set you straight. Amelia will have a great time in the pool and with the horses. I'd love to see you both."

He nodded, feeling lighter. "Thank you. I'm glad I called."

"I am too. If you want to talk—really talk? Call any time, okay?"

"Yeah. Yeah, okay. I will. I'm working up to it." That was the truth. Finally.

"Good. I'm here for you. Let me know when you've made your travel plans."

"I will. Thanks again, Jude. I didn't know who else to call."

"You called the right person. Whatever it is, this is a beautiful place to figure shit out."

"Cool. I'll call again soon."

"Take care, buddy, okay? Goodnight."

"Goodnight." Fox ended the call and set his beer bottle down. "Okay." He took another breath. "Fuck. Okay, that's a plan. We have a plan."

It wasn't much of one. Getting out of New York was the first step, but he had no idea what the second one was.

3

Fuck, it was hot. It was humid.

Sticky.

Trent was hungry. He didn't want to get up off the porch or out of Grampy's old rocking chair because he'd finally just gotten comfortable in this stupid fucking set-up they had his arm in. He looked like a robot.

Trent had come home from Nashville in April, no problem. Wasn't getting home that had been the issue. It was how this damn arm kept getting infected, and he kept having to have surgery. He was just tempted to cut the damn thing off.

Thank God he was left-handed, or he wouldn't even manage to get his own damn jeans off.

As it was, he was spending all his time sitting on the porch watching the grass grow and the hummingbirds at the feeders.

Jesus, was he getting old.

His phone rang, startling the fuck out of him, Rope's ringtone of "On the Road Again" blaring out. He fumbled it out of his pocket, damn near dropping it before he snatched it up. "What do you want?"

"Coming to pick you up in twenty to bring you to supper."

"I'm not hungry." He was starving, but he wasn't going to say so because he didn't want to get up, because he hated everything.

And he was hungry.

"I'll be there in twenty. We got company. Your goddaughter wants to see you anyway."

He couldn't help his smile. That little girl, his little Faith, just had him wrapped around her finger, and she knew it, too.

"What if I say no?"

"You won't. Now get yourself a damn shirt on." Rope didn't even wait to see if he answered. He just hung up. Fucker. Now Trent had to think about how to get out of this chair.

Life wasn't fucking fair.

But what was, right?

By the time Rope showed up, he was dutifully cleaned up and dressed for supper. He'd even shaved for that little baby girl because she needed softer kisses from her god-daddy.

"Hey, Trent. You look great," Jude said as he made his way up the front porch steps, holding onto the railing like an old man. There was one advantage to having supper here: Rope's place had refrigerated air, and Rope's handsome husband didn't look one bit like he was melting.

He really needed to get a new unit, put it at his house, something bigger. He'd bet Rope knew someone.

"Thanks, man. Where's my baby?"

He could say that because he could hear Silas out in the

pool, splashing and jumping around. He learned fast that it hurt Silas's feelings to only ask over the baby, and he got it.

He did.

Silas was a good kid, an exceptional one, and he was one hell of a little cowboy in training.

But Faith was his goddaughter.

He'd never had one of those before. Never seen a brand-new baby and been able to hold her right at the hospital like he was family.

And he *was* family.

Then again, he'd also been at the hospital fixin' to have surgery, so it wasn't like it was a long trip out to Austin.

"She's sleeping. Come on in and sit down. We have company that you need to meet."

Right. Company. "Rope said it was a friend of yours from the city."

He'd discovered that they called it 'the city' like it was the only one ever. Made him feel like he belonged to say it that way, though.

"Mhm. He's having some lemonade." Jude offered him an arm. "Need a hand?"

"Shit, man. I need more than one." He winked at Jude. "Rope wouldn't let me dangle the groceries on the end of my brace, you know…"

"So unfair." Jude chuckled and took him by his good elbow, steadying him a little without being all overprotective about it.

A tall man with neatly combed red hair and a shocking number of freckles on his pale skin stood as they came in.

"Fox, I want you to meet Trent James. He's an old friend —I'm sorry, a long-time friend of Rope's," Jude teased. "Trent, Callum Fox, a good buddy of mine from New York."

"Hey, there. Welcome to Texas. Pleased." He waggled his

fingers, but didn't offer to shake. "Are you enjoying yourself so far, man?"

"I've been here all of one day, but yeah. The ranch is beautiful. We ate like kings last night. Hot as hell though. You want my chair? It's got a good back on it."

"No. No, I'm good." He wasn't going to be rude. No way. This was his best bud's home, and he would never give offense.

"I got you your good chair out on the deck, buddy. I'm fixin' to grill." Rope winked at him, and he followed along.

"Come on, Fox. When Rope says grill, it's not the little Webber you're thinking about," Jude said.

"No?"

Jude chuckled. "Just wait."

They all headed out to the deck, which was under a nice pergola so there was some shade. The shrieks and laughter coming from the pool made him grin.

"Silas has a little girlfriend in the pool, huh?"

There was a soft laugh behind him, and Fox sounded amused. "That's my daughter, Amelia. Don't let her hear you say 'girlfriend'."

"Amelia. I like that name. That was my granny's name." Trent settled right down in the chair that he knew was saved out for him. He couldn't fight his groan as he settled. "Oh, thanks for moving me into the shade, man."

Rope grinned, winked at him. "Anytime, old man, anytime at all. I'm doing country ribs, hot dogs, and I got me a couple of burgers. What you want?"

"Did you get potato salad and coleslaw?"

"Yes, sir. Plus beans, Brown 'N Serves, and Jude made his fancy deviled eggs. There's strawberry shortcake for dessert later."

"Listen to that." Thank God and Greyhound for retirement. "I want ribs, please."

He loved those country ribs with the burning passion of a thousand fiery suns. They were boneless, they ate like a dream, and Rope knew just how to cook them.

"Mr. Fox, what would you like?"

"I gotta say, the ribs do sound great." Fox glanced around and chose a seat on his good side, pulling it up so they could talk without him having to crane his neck. "Amelia loves burgers."

"Beer, guys?" Jude asked, heading for the beer fridge Rope kept on the deck.

"Yeah. I'll take one." He was being conservative with the pain pills. A guy never knew when he might need them.

Jude handed him and Fox a beer. He obviously knew Fox well enough to not need an answer.

"I really do love a beer on a hot day," Fox said.

"What's not to love?" Trent drank deep, letting the icy cold brew splash down into his empty gut. "What y'all been up to, besides getting in my business?"

Rope and Jude had folks coming to clean his house, change his bandages, feed his critters. It was like he was a kept man.

It was notable that Fox hadn't even asked him what he'd done to himself yet.

"Summer is pretty loose around here," Jude said with a snort. "Silas is occupying himself and getting tanned; I'm still working, but it's slow with clients on vacation. And Rope—" Jude shook his head. "I don't even know. I woke up one morning, and he'd bought yaks."

"Yaks?" Fox sounded shocked. "Seriously?"

Trent fluttered his eyelashes. "You do not say? Yaks?"

Rope grinned over at him. "You know what yak butter is going for these days?"

"I hear there's some restaurants down in Austin who are clamoring for it. You taught the boy how to milk a yak yet?"

Jude leaned toward Fox with a grin, but his eyes were on Rope. "Whenever someone says 'yak', Rope reminds us all what yak butter is going for these days. Pay attention. You'll see it."

"You really have a yak?" Fox asked again.

"No, they really have a gnu. We have four yaks."

"Ali, Bebe, Cici, and DeeDee." Silas waved from the pool. "Hey, Uncle Trent."

"Hey, kiddo. How goes it?"

"Good! This is Amelia. She's nice."

"Hello, Uncle Trent!" Amelia parroted, laughing.

Fox sighed. "Sorry. Let me know if you prefer something more polite."

"More polite? Hey, Amelia-girl! Nice to meet you!" Being family was the most polite, wasn't it?

"Well, you know, less..." Fox shrugged. "I don't know. I've only been here a day, but somehow it feels like another planet."

Rope patted Fox's arm. "Jude said that a lot, but my Silas? Not even once. He's our cowboy astronaut to the bone."

Fox nodded. "Amelia slept hard last night so there must be something to all this fresh air."

"Fresh air, goat poop, chlorine—it's all magical." Trent wasn't even being sarcastic.

"Here's to goat poop." Rope held up his beer. Rope understood.

"So," Fox turned in his seat to look at him. "I have to ask you what happened to your shoulder?"

"I had a hell of a wreck in Nashville, and then the new shoulder got infected. It's been a summer."

"A wreck?"

"He's talking about a bull, Fox. Not a car," Jude said, obviously speaking Fox's language better than he did.

"Oh." Fox winced. "Oh, man. You got thrown?"

"Thrown. Trampled. Hooked." He rolled his eyes. "Possibly tap danced on. Twice."

"Jesus. And you've had *how* many surgeries?" Fox leaned back in his chair. "Stop me if I'm asking too many questions, I'm just—I know nothing about bull riding. Well, except what Jude has tried to tell me about how amazing Rope was before he retired."

"He's still pretty damn amazing, just not at bull riding, and seven. It's been great."

Fox blinked at him. "Seven surgeries? That does sound like fun. Are you done yet?"

"Damn, I hope so. I'm ready to get myself back to work. I'm tired of sitting." He needed to be able to feed his damn cows.

"I guess you have a bunch of rehab ahead, huh?" Fox sipped his beer, a blue-eyed gaze shifting between him and the pool.

"That's the rumor. I'm going to have one of those swim spa deals put in, I think. I can exercise in there, relax." Trent wanted to roll his shoulder, so bad. He also wanted to scratch it, deep down.

"Sounds like a great idea if you've got the space, which I assume you do. There's a lot of elbow room out here. I'm not used to that."

"Do you live close to where Jude and them did?" He'd never been inside Jude's old apartment, but they'd all traveled by the last time they were in New York.

"No, actually. I live farther north on the Upper West Side. It's a little bit of a ride to work for me, but I wanted Amelia to be close to her school."

"Ah." That meant absolutely nothing to him, but he was exceptional at smiling and agreeing.

Fox shrugged. "I told you. It's another planet."

Amelia and Silas came wandering up. Silas was happily dripping away, and Amelia was wrapped up tight in a striped towel.

"Hey, sweets. Are you done swimming?"

"I'm all pruney." Amelia held out her hand for her father to investigate.

"You sure are." Fox gave her hand a squeeze. "Time to dry off? Do you want to go change? If you bring me your brush, I'll help with your hair."

"I'm hungry," Silas announced to everyone.

Jude snorted. "Get your towel and dry off, buddy."

"Okay, Daddy. Daddy Rope, can you make me a hot dog? I'm starving." Silas put his hand over his forehead, swaying dramatically. "Wasting away."

Amelia rolled her eyes. "Nobody ever starved waiting five minutes for a hot dog."

Silas hit the deck, arms splayed out to the sides. "Dying."

Amelia bent over him and wrung out her hair, water landing on his stomach.

Silas gasped. "That's cold!"

Amelia ran, and Silas chased her into the house, laughter following them both.

"Don't run in the house!" Jude and Fox called after them.

"Oh, Yankee in stereo!" Trent loved it.

Everyone cracked up, especially Fox, who had the most amazing fit of the giggles.

"Oh, now you've done it, Trent. That was pretty impressive; you've only known him an hour."

"Shut up," Fox managed to say through the giggles.

"You need oxygen yet?" Trent asked.

Fox wheezed. "Shut. Up."

"Ah, the man has a sense of humor. I like that in a neighbor." Trent was tickled. He loved when he made an impression.

Fox just shook his head and took a couple of deep, deep breaths. He stopped giggling but not smiling. "Damn. It's been a while; I needed that laugh."

"Well, I'm tickled shitless I could provide it." He winked over at the guy. It was cool to feel useful.

"Worth the trip down just for the laugh, huh?" Jude hugged Fox's shoulders, and Fox looked sheepish.

"Yeah. Yeah, maybe." Fox sipped his beer again and seemed to sink into his chair a little.

"It works, man. Nothing wrong with letting your friends ease your shit, right?"

NOTHING WRONG WITH FRIENDS.

That was why he was here, right? To be with friends that had nothing to do with his job—his former job—or New York, or anything.

He wondered though, if he might have taken that advice too far. This wasn't New York for sure. It wasn't anything like anywhere he'd ever been. Jude was a good friend, Rope was an outstanding host, but Fox had never felt so completely lost and out of place in his life.

"We all need friends."

He wasn't sure what else to say to that without opening a

door he didn't really want to open. He'd managed to keep the conversation off him so far.

"Rope, this deck is amazing. Do you spend all summer out here?" It had the grill and the pool, but also a fridge and a couple of burners like an outdoor kitchen.

"All summer when I'm not working, yes." Rope grinned over. "I spend a lot of time out in the pasture while Jude watches the boy in the pool and works on his computer."

Jude rolled his eyes. "Ah, yes, I work on my computer. That's what my husband thinks I do for a living."

"He's not totally wrong."

"Who asked you?" Jude shot him a playful look.

"Don't you work on your computer?" Rope honestly seemed confused. "I mean, you have meetings, and you type a lot…"

"Yes, dear." Jude slid an arm around Rope's back and kissed Rope's shoulder. He tried to ignore the little bit of himself that hurt to see that. He was glad that they were happy. He should get over himself.

He was struggling with that. That was why he was here, right?

Trent smiled at him, winked. "They're still newlyweds, but damn they're gooey for new dads."

"Right?" That made him chuckle. He appreciated the wink. "I hear you're the baby's godfather?"

Trent's craggy, tanned face lit up, the greenish-gold eyes dancing. "Miss Faith was born when I was in the hospital. I was one of the first folks to hold her. She's my godgirl."

He loved the pride in Trent's voice. "That's really neat. She's beautiful." She had a set of lungs on her too, but if a baby wasn't keeping her dads on their toes, she wasn't doing her job. At least that was how he remembered it.

"Hot dog?" Silas asked, coming out of the house as fast

as he'd gone in. He was dressed like a mini version of Rope in jeans and a button-down.

Rope arched one eyebrow.

"I mean, can I have a hot dog, please, sir?"

"Sure you can, buddy. Here goes."

Amelia came back in a cotton sundress covered in sunflowers and leaned against him for a second. "Hi, Daddy."

"Hey, sweets." He circled an arm around her waist and gave her a squeeze. "Did you have a good swim?"

"I love their pool. It's so nice."

"I know, right? Are you hungry? I asked Uncle Rope to put a burger on for you."

"Ooh. Yes, please!" She looked up at Rope with that sweet smile she reserved for when she wanted something. "May I please have a cheeseburger, Uncle Rope?"

"Of course you can, honey. Mayo, mustard, ketchup? We also got lettuce, tomato, pickles, onion, and jalapenos."

"Ketchup and lettuce please. Are jalapenos the hot things?" Amelia was a good eater, but she hadn't had any exposure to spicy food.

"They are. They have some kick."

Silas rolled his eyes. "They're *hot*, Amelia. H. O. T."

"Ohh." Amelia looked very serious. "No thank you, then. Just lettuce. Do you have Sprite?"

Jude pointed. "Silas, can you see if there's a Sprite in the cooler?"

Silas dug around in the ice-filled cooler. "There are! Can I have one too, Daddy?"

"Just one, but yes."

He knew Jude preferred Silas not have too much soda. "We don't go away very often. I might be more indulgent than usual."

"Eh. It's summer break, and Silas gets plenty of exercise to wear him out on the ranch." Jude stretched his legs out, grinning. "The move here was so good for him."

"Can we eat by the pool?"

"At the table, not on the deck. Okay?"

"Okay!" Silas led Amelia off to a picnic table.

"Amelia likes it so far." He was happy about that. She needed some fun. Silas was keeping her occupied, so that might give him some time to himself. Time to think.

"She's a sweetheart. Is she in the same grade as Silas?"

"She's a year younger, but she and Silas have... some things in common." Fox wasn't sure if all of that was casual barbecue conversation. "Do you have kids?"

"No, sir. I'm single as the day is long."

"Oh, me too," he answered without thinking. He sipped his beer to cover while he figured out what he was going to say next.

"Yeah? I'm assuming you're into fellers like the rest of us?"

Fellers. Trent was all Texan and so charming it made Fox smile. "Yep. Totally queer."

He was just sitting here with a couple of gay cowboys—and Jude, who didn't seem to have become a cowboy exactly, but fit in just fine anyway.

He knew what Trent was going to ask next, so he answered, if vaguely. "Amelia was born with the help of a surrogate."

"That's cool. She's a beauty." Trent nodded, and he got another of those smiles, warm and easy. "She seems to be having fun, too. You might need another beer. You look worn to the bone."

He snorted softly. He really must look rough if a total stranger was pointing it out. "I am... well, to be truthful, we're here because I needed some time away. I'm exhausted. But I like how you think."

"Help yourself," Jude pointed to the little fridge, and Fox hauled his butt out of his chair.

"Anyone else, while I'm up?"

"I'm good." Jude was never a big drinker.

"I'm a one and done until the pain pills are empty, but thanks."

How did that man just sit there, baking, with God knew what underneath all those bandages?

"Rope? Or am I drinking number two alone?" Wouldn't be the first time. He'd been drinking alone for a long while, and some nights, he didn't stop at two.

"I will so join you. I have light beer. The second one is free." Rope winked at Trent, and they both cracked up.

He laughed. "I like this philosophy." Fox pulled out two beers and handed one off to Rope.

One more beer would help. These were good friends, and he was going to relax and be social and normal for crying out loud. "Those ribs smell incredible."

"I love them—smoked ribs are great, but there's something special about country ribs."

Trent sort of bobbed in agreement. "You know it, man."

"I don't think I'm that well-versed in ribs. But I'll take your word for it. I'm just hungry." Which was something in itself. Fox hadn't bothered to eat a real meal in ages.

"Of course you are. You've been out in the sun and the air. It's good for you." Trent sounded so sure.

He smiled at Trent, which felt strangely good. "I think you Texans might be on to something."

"The whole ranch life thing is a secret of longevity." Trent shot Rope a wicked glance. "Unless you fall under a bull."

Rope snorted. "That does tend to throw a wrench into the long-life deal."

"Or at least a long life without injury." Fox pointed his beer at Trent's shoulder. "Can you go back after... all of that?"

"I could, but I'm not going to. I'm old and tired, and I'm going to raise critters and sell yak butter by the road."

"I hear there's a fortune to be made in yak butter." He winked at Trent and sipped his beer. Trent was beat up, and maybe too old to ride, but he obviously wasn't old. "Seriously though, that sounds like a pretty good idea."

"I hope so." Trent winked over. "I just want to take care of my own shit at the ranch."

"That's going to take some time, man." Rope pointed out.

"Everything takes time," Fox said, sounding more exasperated than he meant to.

"No shit on that, but I'm ready for this nonsense to be done."

"If you need a hand while I'm here, let me know. I don't have any plans." No plans at all. Just hanging out here with the blue sky and the heat and his own stupid thoughts. Although they felt a little less stupid here than they did in New York. Bigger, and yet not. Better and worse. He needed to get his head around it.

"Yeah? You like animals? I don't have as many as Rope, here, but I got a *lot* of chickens..."

"I don't know the first thing about animals, actually. But I am very good at taking directions."

Jude laughed. "No, you're not."

"Okay, fine." He snorted. "I'm not. But I am so willing to pretend I am."

"I can help, Uncle Trent! I can show Amelia how to

gather eggs and feed." Silas popped up like a daisy in the spring.

"That's a great idea," Rope chimed in.

"Chickens?" Amelia's face lit up. "Like real chickens?"

"Like about forty hens, three roosters, and twenty chicks."

"Ooh! Can I, Daddy? Please?" Amelia looked pretty excited about it.

"Of course, why not? As long as it's okay with Trent—uh, Uncle Trent." Instant family. That thought made him grin.

"Of course it is. Y'all are always welcome, and I'd love the help. The front door will be open; just come on in."

That was wild. "I'm from New York. The land of locked *everything*. I'm not sure I'm capable of just walking in."

"We'll knock first," Silas said, so confident. "In case he's peeing or naked."

"Ha!" He laughed so suddenly that he was glad he hadn't just sipped his beer. "Right. Great. Very good idea." And that was it, he was off giggling again. That was twice in the span of an hour, which was twice more than he had in a month.

"Silas! You said peeing!" Amelia whispered, and Silas grinned at her.

"So did you."

Okay. He had to hand it to his therapist. Claire had been right.

This was a good idea.

4

Trent was sitting on his front porch when Silas and the "Rescue the Egg" Committee showed up.

He'd managed frozen biscuits, sausage, and coffee, and Silas could get the orange juice Trent bought just for him.

Goofy kid.

Trent adored him.

"Y'all bring me my baby?" he hollered.

"You know we did!" Jude called back.

"Hi, Uncle Trent!" both kids said at the same time. Amelia had on shorts and a cute pink top, but her boots were ready for work. That girl needed some ranch clothes.

He'd Venmo Rope some money to handle it. He didn't have the slightest idea how to deal with girls' clothes.

Silas was easy. Trent just bought miniature versions of what he liked.

The kids ran right inside. Silas knew where to find everything.

"Did you eat?" Jude was carrying Faith in one arm and a diaper bag in the other.

"Nope. I reckoned I'd wait for you." He took little Faith with his good arm.

Jude helped him get her settled, smiling. "Well, you only have one arm, so you'll have to wait now." Faith blinked up at him. "That's your Uncle Trent, little girl."

"Hey, Angel baby. Hey, Silas," he called. "I got you a new bucket like you wanted."

"He wanted a bucket?"

"Uh-huh. A galvanized one."

Jude looked through the door into the house. "Why did he want a bucket?"

He had no idea. He hadn't asked. "Why does any boy need a bucket?"

"You're a good uncle." Jude patted his shoulder. "Come on, Rope, let's see about breakfast."

"I ordered that orange juice that Silas likes. Hey there, stranger." He called out to Fox. "Come have some food."

The poor guy looked about peaked. Seriously. It was a sad thing, to be so unhappy.

"Oh, hey. Thank you. This is a nice place." Fox trudged up the steps. "How are you feeling today?"

"Like I've been snuggled by a little sweetheart." *Like I got eaten by a bear and tossed up...*

"Isn't she cute? Man, she's a handful though. She's up all night. I don't know how they do it."

"They're madly in love." Up all night? His sweet baby girl? Never.

"That has to be it." Fox bent closer and touched Faith's little nose.

"Yep. They have two amazing kids. Two."

"I've known Silas for a while. He's really something. Curious and outgoing. Amelia loves hanging out with him. She couldn't wait to be here to learn about chickens. I guess she could learn at Jude and Rope's place too, but Rope seems to have a couple of folks that help him out already."

"My place is a lot smaller and way more manageable—barring the unexpected chicks." That had been a surprise.

Fox shrugged. "Well, those you have some willing help with."

"I do! You want to see them?" Poor pretty sad guy. He'd wander them over to the coop.

After he'd gotten his fill of baby Faith.

"Sure, but first, I heard you were making coffee so you sit with her, and I'll get us some."

"No need, I have two coffees and some breakfast for you, Fox." Jude came out with his hands full and handed him things, then set a cup of coffee down on a table for Trent.

"Oh. Food as well. Thank you." Fox sipped his coffee and sighed. "Oh. That's good coffee too. I'm going to gain a hundred pounds the way you all feed me."

"You'll work hard out here. We should all take the boat out, and—"

Jude glared at him. "You are not getting on another boat! You do understand that lake water has germs, right?"

"Picky, picky."

"I'd heard you were your own worst enemy." Fox shot him a snarky grin. "Sounds like the truth."

"I am a bull rider. How could you even doubt?" He shot Fox a shit-eating grin.

"Point taken." Fox took another sip of Trent's perfectly ordinary coffee and hummed. "So good."

"Thank you for the bucket!" Silas and Amelia ran by them, and out toward the chickens.

"You're welcome, kiddo!" See? Buckets were things of joy. "Every boy needs his own bucket."

Jude rolled his eyes. "Maybe. But if he brings something home in it, I will be sure to bring it to you instead."

"Chick-napping?" Fox asked.

"Oh, I don't think he'd bother when he can come here any time he wants." Jude held out his hands. "Would you like to drink your coffee, Uncle Trent? I can take her."

"Baby girl, I am ready to have both hands back, swear to God." He stole another hug.

"Hey, she can hardly hold her own head up yet; she's not gonna judge." Jude lifted Faith from his arms—*arm*.

"But I am. I'm going to fix that leak in the sink." Rope headed to the garage for the toolbox.

"Yeah, yeah. I'm going to show Fox the chicks and check on the kids." That would make him feel less than useless.

"Sounds good. Can I bring my coffee?" Fox stood and offered him a hand up.

"Of course." Trent stood, damn near going ass over teakettle, and it was just his core that kept him upright. "Oops."

Then he noticed Fox's arm around his waist, so maybe it wasn't just his abs after all.

Or maybe he was hallucinating because that touch disappeared so fast it made him wonder if he'd made it up.

"You're good. Just a little wobble."

"Yeah, I'm a little wobbly. It's a thing. Once I get moving, I'm solid as a rock."

"A falling rock!" Rope called as he wandered by.

"A sinking, almost drowning rock," Jude added, like the Yankee asshole he was.

"Firetruck you!" he called.

He grinned smugly at the laughter they left behind.

"You and Rope have been friends a long time, it seems like." Fox fell in on his good side as they walked.

"Long time. We met in junior rodeo. He's my bud."

"Wow. It must be neat to have a friend for that long. I've lost track of everyone from high school."

"Yeah? I bet a place as big as New York City, it has to be hard." He'd bet the high schools had a million people, like the school in *Grease*.

"I went to school in New Jersey, but yeah, it was big. Your high school was small, I guess?" Fox was serious about his coffee, sipping it between sentences.

"Oh, yeah. There were forty people in my graduating class." Maybe. Maybe fewer. He didn't really remember. He'd had a party to go to.

"Forty? That's crazy. I think I had forty people in my homeroom class. That's wild. It's so different here. I'm sure you'd say the same about the city, but I think it a hundred times a day it seems like."

"That's cool. Different is fine, you know? Sometimes you got to escape the same shit and find new stuff." At least that made sense to him...

"Yep. That's exactly what my therapist said. Get out of town, change of scenery, something new, fresh air..." Fox shrugged.

"And here you are, in the middle of dogs and chickens and cows and yaks." Speaking of dogs...

He whistled, knowing that Grissom, Catherine, and Greg would hear him even down in the pasture.

"Is that for the yaks or the—oh. Dogs!" Fox lit up as the pups came running.

The Aussies came barreling up, barking and wagging, but so, so careful of his arm.

"Hey, babies. Meet Mister Fox! Fox, these are the hooligans."

"They're gorgeous." Fox knelt right down where they

could nose him and sniff at him, and he scrubbed their ears and patted their sides. "Look at these guys."

Oh. Good man. Any man who would love on his dogs was good in his book. "They're good guys. Honest."

"I trusted they were, or you would have warned me." Trust. Just like that. Fox squinted up at him. "What are their names?"

"That's Grissom. This little girl is Catherine, and this here is Greg."

"*CSI*. Nice. I have such a crush on Greg." Fox chuckled and stood.

"Yeah? I was into Gary Sinise on the New York one." That man was... hot.

"I read somewhere that he is a nice guy too. I don't watch much TV but Xan—uh. Xan was—" Fox waved his hand like it didn't matter. "Anyway, he got me into *CSI*, and I was hooked."

"Is he... gone or just not in the picture anymore?" Was that any of his business? Probably not.

"Gone." Fox shrugged, then looked his way. "Almost four years now. I don't know why it's still so awkward to tell people."

"I'm sorry. That sucks. You got my condolences." That was awful. Poor guy. Poor baby girl.

"Thanks." Fox snorted and smiled a little. "Anyway, he loved all those forensic-science type shows. He was a lawyer, and he loved to tell me all the stuff they did that would never hold up in court."

"Oh, man. That would be wild. I watch a lot of TV in hotel rooms. A lot." There was always a *Law and Order* or *Forensics Files* on somewhere.

"You travel a lot? I mean, still? Or you mean before?"

"Yes. I did. Before." But that was over. All the way over.

He wasn't big enough to be asked to do a lot of signings or nothing.

"Awful word, right? Before? That line where everything changes."

"I guess, yeah. I mean, now I guess I'm—at the beginning. Soon. Maybe."

Fox nodded. "Maybe me too. I'm trying to get there. I left my job. I couldn't do it anymore, so... time for something new, right?"

"There you go. I'm with you." He'd been retired, sorta forcibly, and he wasn't sure what happened next.

A surprisingly comfortable silence fell between them as they walked. Fox was solid, had a friendly vibe, and made pretty good company.

"Daddy! Come see!" Amelia called to them as they turned the corner and headed toward the chickens. "They're so fuzzy!"

There they were—all these baby chicks that he hadn't had the slightest intention of having. Still, they were adorable.

"Look at that." Fox worked his way around the dogs and followed Amelia to see the chicks. She put one in his hands, and Fox lifted it up for a better look. "Wow. They are definitely fuzzy."

"Aren't they? I'm hoping for hens. I got no need for more roosters."

Amelia blinked up at him. "What will you do if they are?"

"I'll sell them to someone that needs roosters to guard the henhouse. Too many roosters in a coop will fight."

Amelia nodded like this made perfect sense. "Boys. They fight all the time." She grinned at him, and he saw the resemblance between her and Fox in that smile. "I guess you can't send a rooster to detention."

"No, ma'am. They aren't the best at following instructions. They got themselves wee bitty brains."

Amelia's giggle sounded just like Fox's too.

"You're holding Buffy. This one is Fluffy, Stuffy, Huffy, Duffy…"

"No, I think maybe that one is Duffy," Amelia countered.

Silas laughed. "Not anymore!"

"Which one's Puffy?" He managed, just barely, to keep a straight face, but Fox sure didn't. He was laughing good and hard.

"Pick one! They all look the same, Uncle Trent." Silas rolled his eyes, and Fox just laughed even more.

"Yeah, geez, Uncle Trent," Fox said, wheezing.

He snorted. "Y'all make sure they have clean water, okay?"

"How come they have a special waterer? It looks like a bird feeder." Amelia was confused as hell, and Silas was happy to educate her.

"If you give them a bowl, they can fall in and drown. They're just babies, and they're fragile. I have eighteen chickens right now, and three—"

"Show chickens. I know. *Weird*," Amelia piped up.

"Right? It's so cool!"

"Where do you show the chickens off? Do you win stuff if they're the best chickens ever?" Fox asked.

"Well, duh. I get trophies. I get ribbons. Best of all, I get money! I got three hundred dollars for my last hen, Petunia." Silas beamed, so proud of himself. Jude had to be losing it—his astronaut kid showing chickens. "I put half in savings, a hundred dollars to a new coop door, and I got to keep fifty dollars for myself."

"Fifty whole dollars?" Amelia's eyes went wide.

"Yep. I'm going to buy a guitar soon. Me and my buddies are going to start a band."

"I play flute; can I be in your band?"

Fox didn't even flinch.

"You do? For reals? Do they have flutes in country bands, Uncle Trent?"

"Sure. Why not? They have them in folk music..." And this little girl wanted to fit in. What could it hurt?

"Cool! What are you going to name your band?"

And just like that, the kids were off in their own world again.

"My dad used to listen to this rock band that had a lead flautist. I should find it for her on YouTube," Fox glanced at the kids. "He was kind of weird-looking though."

"Oh, weird-looking is damn near normal these days." He winked at Fox, thinking about the wild folks he saw in Austin.

Fox grinned. "You're right about that."

"I can't imagine what will be weird when these guys are grown." It boggled the mind.

Fox shot him a look. "Probably us."

"You're already weird, Daddy." Amelia giggled.

"And there you have it." Fox shook his head. "Want to show me around some more? I'm really not in a hurry to go back and sit down and make more small talk."

"Sure. You got this, Silas?"

"Yes, sir. We'll gather eggs and make sure the chicks are covered and safe."

"Thank you, kiddo." He shot Fox a smile. "You want to see the yaks?"

"How could I possibly refuse?" Fox fell in easily next to

him, seeming more comfortable than he had when they'd arrived.

"There are a dozen of them—two bulls and eight cows and a couple of calves. Four of the others are pregnant."

"Pregnant? Wow." Fox squinted out over the pasture. "Is that them out there? The hairy guys?"

"That's them. Aren't they amazing?" He had to grin. "Fuzzy little f—iretrucks."

Oh, go him!

"Ha!" Fox barked out a laugh. He didn't quite hit the giggles stage this time, but he did flop over and take a deep breath. "Man. I swear I haven't laughed so much in months. *Months*. Thank you."

"It's my pleasure." And that was no lie. It was good to feel useful, helpful, whathaveyou.

"I googled yaks, because Rope kept going on and on about them, and I read that yak meat is more popular than buffalo and you can comb them for fiber. Are you doing any of that?"

"I will, yeah. I mean, right now we're building the herd, but it's in the long-term plan."

"How many do you want? I guess you have plenty of land, huh?" Fox didn't seem to be making small talk, or joking about the yaks like Jude always did. He seemed genuinely interested.

"Well, between me and Rope, we got a bit over a thousand acres, so we have some space." They'd formed a corporation and gone in together on the land around them. They didn't want developers moving in and messing up the way they lived, and there was a tight set of neighbors and ranchers committed to the same thing.

"A thousand?" Fox sounded pretty impressed. "How do you take care of all that land?"

"It's a full-time job, but we manage. There are a handful of guys we use for cowboying, but mostly we do it ourselves." They weren't a big operation, but they had enough.

"Seems like a great job. Working for yourselves, outdoors a lot, dealing with actual animals instead of Wall Street animals." Fox snorted.

"Hell yes." He couldn't imagine. He'd been to New York a couple-three times, and it was big.

Not Sao Paulo big, but damn large.

"Is that what you did? You were a stockbroker?"

"No, the CEO of a private auto insurance company. But the market matters, every damn day." Fox shook his head. "A lot of... stress. Pressure. I don't miss it."

"Ew." His eyes went wide, and he tried to throw his hands up to cover his mouth.

Oh fuck.

Ow.

The world swam for a minute, and he damn near puked from the pain. Bad idea.

Very bad idea.

"Whoa. Trent? What... hey." Fox's arm went around him from his good side, steady and solid. "What happened?"

"Sorry. That pulled." And he was drenched in sweat, shaking like a leaf. "I didn't mean to say that."

"No worries; I quit for a reason." Fox led him over to lean against a fence. "Breathe, man; you're shaking. Deep breath."

"I'm good. Just zigged when I needed to zag, you know?" He did suck in a lungful of air, though, because that was great advice.

"Yeah. That sucks. This contraption they've got you in has to be exhausting."

"You know it, but I kept tearing it open. This is supposed to help." He wasn't sure, but he'd promised Rope he'd try.

"By keeping you from being able to do things you're not supposed to do, I suppose?" He could hear the amusement in Fox's voice. "How's that going?"

"Well... I guess okay, since I have to do everything one-handed..." And it was damn near impossible to sleep, to wash his damn hair, to get off...

"Retirement sounds like it was the right option. But unlike me, I bet you're going to miss it."

"I'm going to miss parts of it, sure. I liked the going and seeing, and I loved some of the guys." The riding? He was getting older every damn day, and it was a young man's sport.

"I guess it's good you have the ranch at least—the land, the animals—I'm not sure what's next for me. I have Amelia... but, what else, you know?"

"You got time, right? You can move. You can hibernate. You can go to the lake and hang out on the boat." That was the best part of being retired.

Fox shrugged. "I guess I better find a lake and a boat."

"Well, I got a boat, Rope's got one, and we share a party barge. Lake's ten minutes down the road. Wanna go?" That sounded amazing—grab the kids, the cooler, and fill it with Cokes, grill some burgers. The kids could play on the slide, he could nap in the sun...

"Soon, maybe. I don't know what Rope and Jude have planned, and anyway, it's my understanding that you're not supposed to get on a boat." Fox started walking again. "You good?"

"Yeah. I'm fine. And I wouldn't get wet in a party barge. I'd just sleep and float." He winked over. No one let him have any fun.

Fox grinned back at him, the sun caught his blue eyes and made his red hair seem even brighter. "Something to look forward to when you get out of that contraption."

"Yeah, yeah, yeah." He pointed with his good hand toward the pasture. "Those are my cattle. The cows, my good bulls, and the steaks on the hoof."

Fox chuckled. "What do you mean by good bulls? They're not steak?"

"The good bulls are proven producers. They make good-sized calves that grow quick. I like to keep a few, but too many are unnecessary." And he was in the organic fancy-assed beef business.

Fox leaned on the fence and sighed. "It's nice here, you know? Quiet. Pretty. You're lucky."

"I am. You know, if you need quiet, you can always come sit over here. No worries." He sat over here a lot.

Fox glanced at him, then looked back out over the pasture. "It's been a while since I shared a house with a baby."

"I got four bedrooms, man. Even if you and the two older kids all came over, you'd be fine." He hadn't bothered to make any of the guest rooms...not guest rooms.

"I could help out around here. I've got two good arms." Fox winked. "I don't want to seem ungrateful to Jude and Rope though, you know?"

"You want me to chat at them? They do have a new baby, after all..." He winked. Poor guy just needed a place to rest and breathe.

"I think I can man up and do it. I'll just tell them it seems like you could really use some help around here." Fox winked right back. "Poor you."

"Yeah, yeah. I'm pitiful, but I got clean beds and each

room's got a TV in it." Silas thought staying at his place was great, in fact. The boy didn't have a TV in his room.

"Cool, I can watch my soaps." Fox grinned at him. "Are you sure you don't mind?"

"Why would I? You have loud parties in the middle of the night?" He was used to rodeo folks coming in and out. He didn't have a pool, but he had quiet and peace.

"Ha." Fox laughed again, and it sounded more genuine every time. "No. I'm not a party guy. But I do like a beer or a margarita once in a while."

"I have a beer fridge, in fact. There's a lot of Ensure in there right now."

"Oh. Yum. I'll pass." Fox rolled his eyes. "Let's go tell my hosts. I'm not sure I'll ever get Amelia away from your chickens anyway."

"Wait until she sees the Angora rabbits."

5

Jude and Rope had been remarkably amiable when Fox suggested he and Amelia stay with Trent for a bit. They were surprised, but also seemed pleased, which was odd because he didn't think he'd been a terrible house guest.

He'd even washed dishes.

But in his more honest moments, he had to admit that Jude was kind and generous to let him stay, but worried and fussed over him so much it had become kind of uncomfortable. In the week or so since he'd arrived, Jude had been keeping him either entertained or busy, and he hadn't had a moment to himself.

He hadn't even seen Trent in the hour since he and Amelia showed up except to be pointed in the direction of the guest rooms.

There was more air in this house, and more elbow room, even though it was smaller than Rope and Jude's place.

Amelia was off somewhere with Silas, and he couldn't have been happier about their fast friendship, she needed it, and Silas was the sweetest kid on earth. That left him on his own, so he decided he'd take a little walk.

Maybe check out the yaks again.

He caught himself grinning about that.

The grass was green and lush, and there were rows and rows of some sort of tree making a fake little street out to a big barn. He headed out that way, allowing himself to just walk.

"Pretty," he said out loud to himself as he strolled along the path with his hands tucked into his pockets. Trent had put some time into making this walk special. He felt like Trent liked details, little things that made bigger things better.

The trees were heavy with... pods. Green pods.

He looked around the base of the tree and found some broken nut shells, oval and deep brown.

Pecans.

These were pecan trees, and there were dozens of them.

"Wow." That was pretty cool. He'd never seen pecans on the tree, but he definitely liked to eat them. He nosed around but didn't see any that looked ripe and figured it must not be time yet.

Everything was so different here. He liked it, but he also felt like he had a lot to learn if he was going to really understand it all.

He moved to the barn, finding a long shotgun building. The front area was a workshop with wood, carefully organized, all sorts of power tools, and a huge workbench with a cradle mostly put together on it.

As he wandered farther, he found four empty, cleaned stalls with watering troughs. After that, there was storage—bags of feed for chickens and horses and cattle, bales of hay, a tack room that smelled of leather and oil. In the very back, there was an ATV parked outside, covered by a short car park.

Now, *that* looked like fun.

He climbed into the driver's seat, just to see what it felt like.

The keys were in it, so he started the vehicle. It was an automatic. How hard could it be?

He probably should ask permission, he was generally a rule-follower, but he felt like Trent would get it. He just wanted to try it out. He found and turned off the parking brakes, then hit the throttle and rolled out of the little covered shed.

He stayed close to the barn and took it slow because he had no idea what he was doing, but even moving slowly was fun. He turned in a circle in one direction, then backtracked and went the other way.

One of the horses came up to the fence, and then, to his utter shock, started copying him. It was as if the beast was playing with him.

After a couple more turns, he stopped and put the brake on again, then slid off the ATV and headed over to the fence. "Hey, there." He reached out and let the horse nose his fingers. That worked with dogs, so he figured it was good for horses too.

It lipped at his fingers, then pushed at his chest, hard.

"She wants a bite of apple." Trent came wandering out. "Hey, Candy girl. I got you covered."

A piece of juicy apple appeared in Trent's hand, and she nibbled it off his palm.

"I knew she wanted *something*." He stroked his hand down Candy's neck. "She was playing with me. I took your

ATV out for a couple of slow circles, and she was doing the circles with me."

"Oh, she's trained to a treat. She'll pretty much do anything you ask her to, and she's bored." Trent grinned at her. "I ought to get you some donkeys to play with."

He figured he'd better start carrying some treats.

"Hope you don't mind me messing with your ATV."

"Hell, no. You're great. You aren't going to break it."

Candy grabbed the hat off Trent's head, backing off and waving it.

"She stole your hat." But without it, he got a better look at Trent. He hadn't realized the man was so handsome.

He was nut brown—tanned skin, brunette hair, with green and brown and gold eyes, which had lovely laugh lines.

Fox stared a bit longer than he'd intended to.

"Come here, Candy." He waved her back over. "Give the cowboy his hat back." It wasn't like Trent was going to chase her.

"Try this." Trent whistled, long and hard, and Candy came right to the gate. "Ta-da!"

Well, that worked. "I don't think I can whistle like that."

"No? My daddy taught me to do it to call horses when I was a kid. It's a handy skill to have."

"Show me how?" He immediately regretted asking. He sounded like a kid.

"Absolutely. I'd love to." Trent winked at him. "Stick your fingers against your tongue, squeeze the corners of your mouth, and blow."

He copied what Trent was doing and tried it, mostly just making a fool out of himself. He tried a couple more times and got the idea but not the whistle. He smiled sheepishly. "Something to work on."

"There you go. The first time it works, you're going to scare the hell out of yourself." Trent didn't seem the slightest bit concerned or embarrassed.

His phone buzzed, and it was Jude.

JUDE

The neighbors are taking a van full of kids to the movies @5. Can A go?

"Oh. Cool." He smiled and texted back.

FOX

She would love that. I'll bring the kids over in time. They're around here somewhere.

"Kids are going to the movies later."

"Good on them. I'm seriously considering watching TV and dreaming about burgers."

"I'm pretty sure I can manage to make a cheeseburger if you want one." He was a fan of binging things on TV too.

"Yeah? Hell, man. I'll give you my truck keys if you want to get a couple in town." Trent sounded almost desperate.

"I can do that. That sounds pretty good actually. Easy. I've got my rental. I'm going to take the kids over to Jude and Rope's later, and I'll head into town after that. I just need the name of the place you want me to go." He had GPS. He'd find it. And he liked the idea of an adventure into town. He hadn't been there yet.

"The Dairy Dart. They have the best onion rings on earth." Trent grinned at him. "That would rock. I'll buy."

"Oh, no. I'm staying rent free in your space. Dinner is on me." Candy nibbled at his shoulder, and he reached out and stroked her neck. "Including a mountain of onion rings."

"Uhn. Yes, please. Thank you." That was a sex noise if he'd ever heard one.

He was kind of surprised he recognized it; he hadn't heard one in a long while. "Next best thing to an orgasm, huh?"

"Man, I'm so fucking tired of Ensure, and I'm retired! I can eat!"

Ensure. Trent said his beer fridge was full of it. "Is that all you've been eating?" His eyes went wide, and he knew he was gaping, but seriously, a man needed cheeseburgers.

"Unless I'm next door, pretty much. I ain't a great cook, but grilling takes two hands, you know?"

Well, he knew what his job was for now. He had to eat too, right? "I got you covered. I'm not a gourmet chef, but I know my way around a kitchen. I have a kid, so I have to. No more Ensure for you. Yuck." It was the least he could do for Trent for allowing him and Amelia to stay for a while.

"Yeah? I don't need fancy, and I can buy groceries and all, but I'd love real supper." Trent offered him a warm, happy smile that felt damn good.

It was pretty cute on the cowboy too.

"Good because I don't do fancy. I do whatever Amelia will eat and spice it up a bit for myself. I haven't grilled much, but I'm game."

"No? Do you not like it?" Trent looked so confused, and it was weirdly adorable.

"I love it. I don't have a grill in the city. Very few people do because of all the fire safety laws. You're used to a lot more space here."

"Oh, God yes." Trent leaned against the fence post. "I been a couple of times. It's overwhelming, a little, the way y'all live one on top of the other. Fascinating."

He nodded. Overwhelming was the story of his life. It was all too much. "It is that. I've lived there a long time.

Married Xan there, had Amelia. You'd think I'd think more fondly of the place than I do right now."

"Well, I reckon there's some real hard memories. It sounds like you needed something brand new."

"That's what everyone says." Literally everyone. "Go somewhere, get out of the city, get a change of scenery, try something new, meet new people." He winked at Trent. "I guess I can check all of that off now. I picked the right place."

"Yep. Now you got new friends, a new set of kids for Amelia, and the need to learn how to whistle."

He tried again with no luck. "I'm going to get it. You'll see." He helped Trent get steady after leaning against the fence, and they headed back toward the house. "I love the pecan trees along the walkway. So pretty, all that green."

"They'll start dropping in late August, early September. I'll have to pay all the neighbor kids to come harvest for me."

"Amelia will love that. She and Silas can organize it, and we can have a little party." He blinked at Trent. First of all, what was he thinking, and secondly, what was he *thinking*? "Uh. Well, we probably won't be here actually, but it sounded like fun."

"It will be, and you ain't got to do a thing but breathe right now and love on your little girl. No stress." Trent grinned at him, nice and easy.

That was true. He was all about reconnecting with Amelia. He didn't feel stressed. He'd just remembered for a moment that he had no job and no plan beyond waking up here tomorrow. It wasn't as stressful as it was weird. "And learn to whistle."

"That's super crazy important. Whistling and watching

movies while the kids make mud puddles." Trent winked at him.

He felt himself smile again and knew it was a quirky one. "Thank goodness Amelia is as into mud puddles as she is into dresses and nail polish." His girl would rock jeans and party dresses equally well.

"So she seems to be happy out here. She's so curious and bright. I don't see how you keep up with her."

That made him smile. Trent didn't need to notice kids, but he saw Amelia. Trent paid attention. "She's going to fly right by me one day, I'm sure. She just loves learning anything. Everything."

He liked to think she'd gotten that from him.

"That and reading are the two biggest things she can have. Good on her. Are you a reader?"

He nodded. "I read. Not as much as I'd like to, but I do. And I read with Amelia a lot too." Amelia liked all kinds of books.

"I like some stories a lot, some I don't. What do y'all like? I don't got any little girl books here, but there's a small library..." Trent moved to sit in the ATV. "You can drive."

He nodded, grinning. "Seems like the best idea." He started it up again, and they rolled slowly toward the house. "I'll take her to the library. That's a great idea. Maybe we'll go tomorrow and then hit the market for some groceries."

"Sounds good. It's not big, but it's got the basics— jalapenos, tomatoes, tortillas..."

"Ground beef? Pasta? Chicken nuggets? I'm not sure Amelia will survive without macaroni and cheese and chicken nuggets."

"Mac and cheese is proof there's a God, man." Trent nodded happily. "And I'll eat all that. You don't ever need to buy meat or chicken, though. It's in the chest freezer."

"Oh. Right. Farm." He pulled up in front of the house and put on the brake. "Door to door service. Hope the ride wasn't too bouncy for that arm."

"You did fine. It was a good—"

"Daddy!"

"Uncle Trent!"

"Look what we found!"

"Can we keep them?"

Trent grinned. "Oh fuck."

"Oh. Uh..." He glanced at Trent, then they headed over, and there was a litter of squirming little mewling kittens. "You have barn cats? Isn't that a thing?"

"I have, but I try to keep them fixed, and I give them their shots. I don't want a bunch of feral cats spreading disease."

"We can get them fixed!"

"And shots!" Amelia said carrying two—or wait, maybe three—kittens in her arm.

"Is that all of them? Maybe we should take them to a shelter?" That's what people did in the city anyway.

"Well... let's call the doc. He'll tell us what they need. Call your dad, Silas. See how many he wants." Trent rolled his head on his neck. "And you have to talk to your daddy about keeping some, little bit. It's a lot of work."

Amelia turned her big eyes on him. "I can do it, Daddy. I promise."

He shook his head. He felt bad, but he couldn't say yes. "I know you can, but we can't have pets in New York, honey." He'd like to say yes, but his building was service animals only. "You can help take care of any kittens that Silas is allowed to keep while we're here though."

"Don't you need some kittens, Uncle Trent? That way they can be Amelia's Texas kittens." Silas's eyes were huge, willing Trent to say yes, and Fox knew, at that moment, he was fucked.

He sighed and shrugged at Trent. "I'll cover the doc visit and the shots and everything." And neuter them when it came time, and... whatever else Amelia asked him to do because he was *that* dad.

Trent chuckled softly. "I'll do the shots, but sure. You two figure this out—about how many go where, get them some food and water, all that. I'll call Doc Trimble. Fair?"

"Okay! Thank you, Uncle Trent!" Silas leaned in Trent's direction, arms full of kittens. "Can we put them in a stall for now? While we call Daddy and all?"

"Go get that box out of the mud room and put some towels in it and put them in the mud room. Shut the screen door so the dogs don't get at them, just in case." Trent looked so tired, almost bruised now.

"Okay. Come on, Amelia." Silas hurried off with Amelia at his heels.

"Ready to head inside?" Trent looked set up for a nap. Poor guy. "Maybe some pain meds or something?" He climbed out of the ATV and went around to help Trent out.

"Yeah, after I help Frick and Frack there, I'll totally crash for a few."

"I can deal with the kittens, Uncle Trent. I swear!"

"Me too!" Amelia was going to shake apart.

"I can handle it. They're kittens, not yaks." Fox pretended not to notice Trent wince as his feet hit the ground. "You crash, and when you wake up, kittens will be sorted and burgers will be on the way."

Trent looked utterly confused. "You sure, man?"

He figured Trent wasn't used to people around to help. "Sure. I got this. You look like you're ready to fall over."

"It's been a long day. Let me get you come cash for supper and gas."

Trent was adorable, taking care of him.

He followed Trent inside without arguing, even though he had no intention of using Trent's money. Dinner was the least he could do.

Trent seemed like he could probably use a little taking care of himself.

6

"Trent. Buddy. I got our supper. Sorry I was so late. I hit the grocery store and picked up things for here and a few things from Jude's."

Trent blinked, trying to remember where he was. He'd been dreaming about Hawaii, about beaches and pretty men.

"I do like pretty men." He smiled and sat up.

Fox damn near tripped over his own feet. "You don't say?"

"Sorry. Sorry, I was dreaming about... dreaming." He lifted the bottom of his T-shirt and wiped his face from where he had been sweating. "Sorry. Burgers smell good."

"They really do." Fox hesitated for a second, then offered him a hand up. "Ready to eat?"

"Totally. I'm so in." He stood up, his shoulder still being quiet. He was so in. "Was the store okay for you?"

It wasn't a big HEB or nothing, but it was just fine.

"It was perfect. I didn't recognize some of the brands, but it got the job done. Your fridge was empty. Like, really empty. I'll be able to make a couple of meals now."

"I'll show you where the big freezer is too. There's chicken, turkey, cabrito, beef. Whatever you want." He was curious to know what all Fox had bought, but he needed those onion rings.

"No rush. Right now, I want that cheeseburger. Come on." Fox led the way to the back porch where there were burgers, onion rings, and Cokes.

And a box of kittens.

Six. He was going to have to set them up somewhere. Maybe the laundry room. He'd worry about it after food.

Fox opened his Coke for him and sat down. "I guess you had a good nap, huh? Sorry I woke you, but I figured this was better hot."

"No. No, that's fine. I'm glad." He was starving, and this was perfect. "Did they give you any ranch?"

"Yes. I thought it was odd but..." Fox handed it over. "You need me to cut that burger or anything?"

Weird? That he was glad or the burger? "What part? And please. I got to manage it one-handed."

"Ranch. On burgers." Fox must have been thinking about him because he picked up a knife that was already on the table.

"It's for the onion rings." Silly man. Although he could dip his burger.

Fox tilted his head as he cut the burger into something Trent could pick up one-handed. "Still weird. But... I might try it."

"Did you get something to dip your rings in then?" He didn't know if he had anything besides ranch... "And you can have as much as you want."

"Yeah, ketchup. All good." Fox opened up his own burger. "Oh, man. This looks so good. Eat up. I know you're hungry."

He got the half burger up and chowed down. It was a little messy, and he had to struggle some, but it tasted so damn good.

"M-mm. You're right, this is delicious." Fox took another bite and closed his eyes. "Mmm."

Okay, that was awful pretty. He could watch Fox's lips for hours, he swore. They made his eyes cross some.

Fox chewed for a bit, then chuckled as he put his burger down. "This is going to sound stupid, but I'm not sure I've ever slowed down enough to really enjoy a burger."

"That's a shame. I do love me a burger, man. Swear to God." And this was the best one in a month of Sundays.

"Amelia is also a fan of a cheeseburger. You look a little like you could use to eat a few more." Fox winked at him.

"Ensure. It's the fucking bane of my existence. Still, it's easy, and it's calories, right?" And he didn't have to ponder on it too hard.

"I suppose." Fox picked up an onion ring. "It's not a cheeseburger. Or tacos. Or spaghetti and meatballs."

"Lasagna. King Ranch casserole. Frito chili pie." He loved all of the above.

"Oh." Fox's eyes went wide. "You're going to have to teach me about Frito chili pie."

"You don't know it? Damn, you have been neglected. I'll help."

Frito chili pie—no matter how someone did it—was necessary.

"Excellent. Who doesn't love Fritos?" Fox chomped on an onion ring. "This is nice. Easy. I mean, Jude is great and really kind to let us stay, but dinner is a whole production over there."

"Lord yes. There's my godgirl, plus working around whatever the boy has, and God help him, Rope's decided to become a damn foodie." It made no sense, but it was what it was.

"Right? And everyone has to sit together and... use a fork." Fox looked at him like that was the most ridiculous idea ever, but he couldn't hold a straight face for long.

"You forgot about the 'ask about your day' thing, which given that they work from home most of the time..."

Fox laughed softly. "Silas is the only one who ever says anything interesting."

"Yes, but that's almost always about pooping or outer space. What all does your girl like talking about?" He wasn't sure what all she was into—crayons, for sure.

Fox squinted at him. "I'm not sure." He got a shrug. "I've been a little distracted. She likes music, books, ponies, her hair... girl stuff, I guess."

"Ah. I like horses and music, but my hair? My glorious mane?" He amused the fuck out of himself.

There was that happy giggle again. "Not that anyone ever gets to see your flowing locks, since you hide them under that hat. I hadn't even really seen your eyes until Candy snatched it off your head. They have little flecks of gold that reflect in the sunlight."

Trent's cheeks heated, and his belly tugged a little, deep inside. No one ever commented on his eyes. "I got those from my momma. She was a beauty pageant queen, believe it or not."

Fox swallowed before he spoke and picked up his Coke. "Oh yeah?"

"Uh-huh. She did all the little ones, and she was even Miss Rodeo Texas. She's beautiful, and my daddy adores her." They were good folks. Solid. They tried to understand him, and he reckoned that he was a little easier than his sister who was a scientist who worked ninety hours a week, didn't wear makeup, and refused to get married and have babies.

Fox blinked at him for a second and then blinked again like he'd just remembered they were having a conversation. "Oh. Cool. Are they local? You'll have to show me a picture sometime when we aren't covered in gooey cheeseburgers."

"Local-ish. They're in Wimberley, which is about as far south from Austin as we are north, but they're in Ruidoso for the summer. They go every year." And thank God for that. Momma could hover.

"Mountains, I assume? I love the mountains. Xan and I used to go up to Tanglewood every summer. There was a big music festival up there. It was fun."

"Ruidoso's real pretty, nice skiing. My folks have a house there." He liked to go in the shoulder season and just watch the critters.

"Nice." Fox groaned and leaned back in his chair. "I am so full. That was just what I needed."

"Hell, yes. I feel like a python that swallowed a rhinoceros." He patted his belly, so happy.

"That sounds painful." Fox smiled at him. "I'll clean up as soon as I can move again."

"Mmhmm..." He might just stay in this deck chair for the rest of his life.

Fox looked out over the back and sighed. "How long have you had this place?"

"I bought it from Rope before his dad died. This was his, and he expected to get the land from his mom, buy her out, but she wanted it sold."

"Huh. Families are complicated, right? It's a great piece of land. So many acres." Fox shook his head. "I've never known anyone who owned so much... earth."

"No?" That made him a little proud. "Thank you. I love it here. I said, when I bought it, I'm retiring right here."

"I would too, if I owned anything anywhere near this beautiful." Fox sighed, but it wasn't long-suffering, it was strangely hopeful sounding. "Maybe I will."

"I can see it." There was a hint of cowboy in Fox. Trent felt it in his balls. It wasn't big—a sparkle—but it was bright.

Fox started cleaning up. "So how many kittens are you stuck with?"

"Two. Jude took one, but that was enough for him. I told Amelia she could name them." That seemed to blow her little mind. She'd filled him in on the whole deal after his nap, and they'd made the call.

"That was nice of you. I bet she was excited. We can't have pets in our building in New York, and she loves animals. Just loves them."

"She was tickled as hell. It was cute as all get out. She couldn't decide. She was torn between Peach and Piggie-Pie or Mouse and Monkey."

"How in the world did she come up with those?" Fox chuckled and gathered up all the trash. There weren't many leftovers. "You stay here; I'll be right back."

Like he was ever going to be able to move.

Ever.

"I'm assuming they were friends from New York?" Trent called, teasing.

"I'm going to have to ask!" A couple of minutes later, Fox was back again, playfully waddling through the back door. "I feel like a moose."

He made what he hoped was a passable moose noise, assuming that Fox wouldn't know if he was wrong. He got a stare, and then a hearty laugh in return.

"Wow. That was… wow." Fox giggled and started to sit and then froze. "Uh. That looks like a big storm, huh?"

He looked over his shoulder, frowning. There was one hell of a gully washer, complete with lightning rumbling from the west.

"Yeah, let's get the dogs in. The lanterns are in the emergency closet."

Fox went right to him, offering to help get him out of his chair. "Sounds good. You want me to take that ATV back to the shed?"

"Can you pull it out there under the car park? That'll work. You ain't got much time. I'm going to whistle up the dogs."

"I'm on it." Fox helped him get to his feet, which he hadn't asked for but sure made things easier, then hurried off and the first clap of thunder rumbled through.

The dogs came at his whistle, barreling into the house, a mass of teeth and tails, damn near bowling him over.

The heavens opened up, and the rain came down hard enough that the ATV was just a blur from where he was standing. Then Fox appeared, running full-tilt for the house with a big grin on his face.

"Come on! Run, Foxy! Run!" Trent cracked up, slapping his hand on his thigh in applause.

Fox bounded up the steps two at a time and landed two-footed on the front porch, laughing. "Whoo! That's some weather." Fox shook his head like a dog might, water flying.

He laughed, his body wanting to firm up, to respond. Probably not appropriate, but he was glad to feel things working…

"God, I'm soaked. At least it's not cold. Did you hear that thunder?" Fox's eyes were bright, and somehow, he seemed taller, stronger.

"Yep. Lightning storm's coming. Wanna watch?" He was totally into it.

Fox lifted his T-shirt and gave it a twist, wringing out the water and showing off tight abs and a dark trail of hair. "Definitely. There's so much more sky here than at home."

"Yeah? It's going to be a show. I can tell." He leaned against the front porch railing and ogled a little bit.

"If you're lucky enough to be high up, you can see pretty far in New York, but otherwise, the sky view is limited, you know?" Fox came over and leaned his shoulder against a post. "You okay? You want to sit?"

"I'm good. There—" He grinned. "Look! There it goes!"

The lightning chased itself through the clouds, bright then dark.

"Woo! That's so cool. I love a summer storm." Fox ran his hands through his hair, taming it.

"Me too. This is one of my favorite things, ever." He was a weather fan—it didn't matter. He loved being outside in this.

"I wonder—my phone's dry." Fox pulled his phone out of his pocket and started scrolling. "Amelia's not great with thunder. But I don't see a text or anything, so I guess she's okay."

"Aww... well, she's in good hands, and if she's in the movie theater, she'll never even know."

"That's what I'm hoping." Fox nodded, putting his phone away. "She's really loving her time here. She missed Si— whoa!" Fox grinned as the sky put on another show.

He hooted, watching the sheets of rain just soaking the ground.

"So the animals are all okay out in this weather?" Fox stuck his hand out into the rain, letting it bounce off his fingers.

"Yeah, they're built for it." And the chicks were in the coop, thank God.

"Are you built for it?" Fox shot him a grin and a wink.

"Weather? I have been in everything minus a... a... what do you call them things where it's an underwater earthquake and the big waves come?" It wasn't a typhoon...

"A tsunami?" Fox laughed. "I was teasing, but I haven't been in one of those either. Or a tornado. No, thank you."

"I've been through a shit-ton of those. Fascinating damn things." He checked the sky. No green, they were solid there.

Fox raised an eyebrow. "That's one way to look at it, I guess."

"Well, it's true, yeah? They're truly wild. Better than any bull ride." And he was into it.

"Possibly even more likely to kill you though." Fox grunted and toed off his shoes. "Ugh. Okay I need something dry. You mind if I run and change?"

"Not at all. I'm going to sit and enjoy the cooler weather." He headed across the porch, getting out of the worst of the rain. Then he sat and propped his arm up, leaning back in the big chair, noting that Fox was waiting to make sure he hadn't gone ass over teakettle.

Lord, that man was pretty enough to ogle.

"Cool." Fox tugged his wet T-shirt off over his head and hung it over the porch railing. Under the fuzzy chest, Fox was paler than most guys Trent knew, but he was in decent shape for someone who didn't work with his hands all day. "I'll be right back."

The man's freckled skin was more obvious on his back as he walked away.

"I'll be right here." Just filing those images away to use late at night for a moment of happiness. He still had one good hand.

7

Okay, maybe taking off his shirt hadn't been the best idea.

Fox hadn't taken his shirt off in front of another man in years, not even at the gym, and he probably shouldn't have done it just now either.

He wasn't sure what he'd been thinking. Trent was fun for sure, and Fox hadn't laughed so much in ages. He felt lighter around the guy. Easy. He felt... more like himself.

The warmth in Trent's smile made him feel kind of sexy, and he'd felt like flirting a little.

For fun, that was all.

He snorted at himself. He hadn't totally forgotten how to have some fun after all.

He found dry jeans and a clean T-shirt. He ran his fingers through his hair, not that it did any good because it did whatever it wanted to anyway. Then he grabbed his wet jeans and headed back out to the porch.

Trent was splayed out, eyes on the water, country music playing from his phone. That belly was amazing—flat and hard, ripped.

He watched for a second, taking in the whole picture but especially those abs before moving to the railing to hang his pants beside his T-shirt. He didn't know much country music, but he liked the vibe. "You look comfy. Mostly." He couldn't imagine that arm was ever comfortable.

"I am comfy. Mostly." Trent winked at him, drawl slow and sweet. "You feel better?"

He dragged a chair over and settled in. "I'm dry. My kid is being looked after somewhere else, and I'm sitting here with you, so yeah. I'm good."

"There's beer in the beer cooler. Cokes too." Trent laughed as a couple of calves went galumphing across the pasture, kicking their heels and bellowing.

"I thought it was full of Ensure?" He wasn't going to ask, since Trent couldn't drink, but he grabbed himself a beer since it had been offered.

"I had Rope stop at the beer store for you. He knew your favorites."

"That was thoughtful. Thank you."

He settled in his seat again, stretching his feet out in front of him. They watched the animals for a bit, and a comfortable silence settled between them while he sipped his beer.

"So... how did you get into rodeo?"

"My daddy, I guess? I mean, I grew up around rodeo. I was never intended to be anything else."

He couldn't imagine that. People just didn't grow up wanting to be in rodeo.

"Nothing else? Ever?" He'd had so many ideas. He hadn't ever really decided. After college, he'd just kept trying one new job after another until he'd ended up in New York.

"Nope. I wanted to be in the big show—hearing the

cheering and being under the lights." Trent gave him a glinting grin. "The hot Wrangler butts didn't hurt."

"Huh." He chuckled. He'd been a football fan for the same reason once. "You know, I hadn't given much thought to them until just now. But maybe I should pay more attention."

"Wrangler butts? They're something special..." That was a wicked wink.

For a second, he tried to picture Rope's butt, but then he decided that was way too sleazy. "I'll have to get a better look when you stand up again."

Yep. He said that.

Damn.

"Fair enough." He didn't get so much as a blink. Not a blush. Just a naughty little nod. "These aren't my best jeans, but they fit."

"I'm just curious how you got them on." He sipped his beer and relaxed, enjoying how Trent just played along with him.

"It took about an hour, but they're on." Trent waggled his eyebrows. "I can't wait to have both hands back."

That made him swallow. He had to believe Trent was good with those hands. "I bet. You'll be able to open a beer."

"I'll be able to take a real shower. I'll be able to go swimming. I'll be able to put on a shirt by myself."

"Things to look forward to." That brace thing had to suck. He'd probably never have to find out; he didn't have enough daredevil in him to get that injured. He leaned toward the edge of the porch. "I think the rain is letting up."

"Yep. There's another round coming in about half an hour." Trent tried to roll that shoulder, and Fox could hear the straps groaning. "Gonna be a wet night."

"I guess that's rough on your bad arm, huh?" He had a

tricky knee, but it didn't seem to be bothering him nearly as much here as it had in the city for some reason.

"Not as bad as it will be in ten years, huh? That's when it'll be brutal, and I'll cry." Trent winked over at him. "Now it itches like a bitch."

Cry. Ha. He rolled his eyes. "You do not strike me as a crier." Itching was the worst. "Like, an inside itch or an outside itch? I could maybe put something on it for you." What? God, he'd just meant that to be helpful and it came out... hot. "I mean—if it would help."

"You mean it? Because I got this cream stuff. But I got to tell you, it's ugly, so if you're squeamish..."

"Oh, you got me. I'm a delicate flower." He shrugged and batted his eyelashes at Trent.

"Don't make me blow kisses at you now." Trent chuckled. "I'd love a little relief, man. And I'm not talking about my dick."

"Well, thank God for that. Someone might think you're gay."

"God for-fucking-bid. I much prefer fudge packer." Trent laid that out without a hint of expression.

He snorted and set his beer down on the railing. "Oh, I'm sorry. I didn't mean to offend. Can I get that cream for you, Mr. Fudgepacker?"

"That's Señor Dick-Sucking Fudgepacker to you." Then Trent cracked up, just howling with joy. "It's in my bathroom on the counter. It's a prescription tube, not the lube."

He laughed along, really enjoying the banter. "Jesus, I'm glad you told me. It's been so long I think I've forgotten what lube looks like." He wandered off saying, "prescription, not lube," over and over, loud enough for Trent to hear, grinning like a fool as the laughter followed him through the house.

The big living room-kitchen-dining room split off in two

directions—one went to the three smaller bedrooms, and the other went toward Trent's room. He followed the hall, not worrying at all about feeling awkward wandering into Trent's bedroom until he got there.

You didn't just wander into your host's private space, let alone into his bathroom. That was nosy and weird.

Especially if your host was a hot, if slightly beat-up, cowboy.

But here he was, pretending not to notice anything as he moved past the man's bed toward the bathroom.

What he did notice was that the bed was made, and there was a recliner in the room that wasn't meant to be there. Also, it smelled just like Trent, and someone needed help with his laundry.

God, he couldn't imagine having to sleep in a recliner every night. Although, even as he thought that he remembered sleeping on the couch for a year after Xan had died. Not the same thing, but a guy did what he needed to do, right?

He'd get Trent all relaxed and then he'd start some laundry. He could make himself useful; he didn't mind. He kind of liked it actually—being able to help the guy out.

The bathroom was a good size, and he found the cream easily. There was no lube anywhere near it, which made him laugh enough that it echoed against the tiled walls of the shower.

Funny guy.

There were towels in the bathroom, and a note on the mirror. "Call and ask me for help, asshole. R."

That was telling, and also so like Rope. He was a good guy, so perfect for Jude, although no one would ever think so just to look at them. Rope was generous to a fault, and apparently as good a friend as he was a husband.

Fox grabbed the prescription and headed back through the bedroom. He stopped by the hamper and pulled the bag out, figuring the laundry was probably somewhere near the kitchen.

He was going to have to do his own laundry soon enough anyway.

There was a nice laundry room off the kitchen, with a hanging rack, a folding table, and a bunch of boots and hats and jackets.

Score. He separated out the laundry, being very adult about sorting out undies and socks, and put in a white load, figuring those were the things a man would run out of first.

"I found it," he said as he stepped back out onto the porch. "And I set up a load of laundry for you."

"Oh, you rock, man. You didn't have to do that. Thank you." Trent blushed, and it was so pretty.

He was glad he'd done it; that blush was worth his time. "I have a daughter. I do a lot of laundry. It's all good."

"Still, I appreciate it, man. Now, I need to unstrap enough to get my shirt off." Trent didn't look super enthused.

"Okay, tell me what to do." This had to be easier with two people. "Start up here by the shoulder, or down by your waist?"

"We're just going to unstrap the shoulder—go slow. Then we jury-rigged me up Velcro shirtsleeves, so you can pull me open."

"Velcro shirts. Clever." He found the strap on the shoulder and started to loosen it very slowly, watching Trent's face to make sure everything was okay. "How's that? Slow enough? You good?"

"Yeah. Any pain will be worth it to get some relief from the itch." Trent was beginning to sweat on his upper lip.

"Okay, let's see if I can get that shirt loose without doing too much more." He reached for the sleeve and tugged at the Velcro, trying not to jostle Trent's shoulder more than he had to.

The bandage came away with the shirt, and Jesus, it was raw and red and painful looking. Trent had to be in agony.

"I hope they have you on the good meds." He'd never seen anything like it. He didn't know how Trent wasn't in the hospital.

"I try to only take one at night. I got to be functional. It's still looking okay, right?"

There was nothing—nothing—about this that was okay.

"Um. Well, it doesn't look infected." Hopefully, that would satisfy Trent because otherwise it kind of looked awful, and he didn't want to say so. And he'd just volunteered to put some of this cream on it.

"Good. Good. Thanks for this."

Oh God, he needed to wash his hands. "Before I touch it, I should probably—I was eating that burger, and my hands are—I'll be right back." That would buy him two minutes to get it together.

He headed off, and he forced himself to breathe. Trent was coping. All he had to do was put goo on the damn thing. It was probably so red because of the seams and Velcro.

He washed his hands and thought about how he was going to help Trent be more comfortable. He just hoped he didn't hurt anything while he was at it.

Man up. He was a big boy.

"Okay. All cleaned up."

"I'm sorry, man. I know it's gross. I just—It itches so fucking bad." Trent had worked the lid off the cream, but he just couldn't quite reach.

"Nope. Don't apologize, you're good. I'm happy to help."

He took the cream and dipped his fingers in it. "Just slather it on? Should I work it in?"

"Just slather it on. Don't mind me if I make a noise. I'm okay."

He huffed a short laugh. "So ignore the wild voice begging me to stop?" He got to work as gently but as quickly as he could manage, figuring it was best not to take his time.

It shocked the hell out of him to see Trent's eyes fill with tears, cheeks flushed. He didn't acknowledge it though, just did his best to get the cream on nice and even everywhere, telling himself it was good for the cowboy in long run.

"Okay. I'm done. All done, cowboy." He put the cap on the cream and set it aside, then wiped his hand off on his wet jeans hanging on the railing since he was going to wash them anyway. He rested a hand on Trent's good shoulder, giving it a little squeeze of comfort.

"Oh. Oh, so much better. Thank you." Trent wiped sweat off his forehead.

Poor guy. Better and worse. "Can I get you some water or something? Pills?"

"No. No, I'm good. Sprite? Can I have a Sprite?"

"Oh yeah. Now you're living large." He slid over to the porch fridge and grabbed one, opening it as he headed back. He figured he could lighten things up a bit. "One Sprite. Go easy. That shit'll go to your head."

"Those bubbles are a scary damn thing."

He appreciated Trent's attempt at a grin. "Let me know when you're ready to get all strapped in again."

"Yeah. I'll give it a minute to breathe. I don't need much, but I want it to get some air."

"Makes sense." He sat again, so he didn't seem like he was hovering, even though that shoulder looked like a reason to hover. "So you did that how long ago?"

"Three days before little bit was born. So April. Damn near three and half months." Trent sighed. "It got infected real bad, then they replaced the joint. That's the scar in the front. The top's from where they scraped out the rot."

"Yikes." He winced and picked up his beer again. "Rope made it sound like you weren't the best patient, but I'm not sure I would be either. Man."

His phone started to play in his pocket, and he pulled it out. "Amelia's texting. It's some Taylor Swift song she put on there." He looked at the text.

AMELIA

daddy can i stay the nite with my new friends? silas says i can borrow pjs

He grinned at that. Look at his little girl, making friends and having a sleepover.

FOX

At Uncle Jude's house?

AMELIA

yes with other people that we went to the movie with

FOX

Sure. Tell Uncle Jude I'll call later.

AMELIA

THANK YOU. YOU ARE THE BEST DADDY EVER

That was followed by a million rainbow hearts.

Pages of them.

"She's staying the night. Silas is lending her PJs."

"Oh, wow. Is this her first sleepover?" Trent actually seemed interested.

"No, but I love that she feels comfortable and is making some friends here." He shrugged. "I just want her to be happy, you know?"

"Sure. Of course. This is a great place to be a kid. When Silas got here the first day, I was here, and he told his daddy he wasn't ever going back."

"It seems like he was born here. Amelia is learning a lot from him. I wouldn't be surprised if she told me the same thing soon." He wasn't sure what his answer would be either. Maybe he'd even say yes. Maybe.

"You think? That would be something. I know that there's not as much to do here, but it's way different from where you were."

"I don't know; for a kid, there's a lot to do. Maybe more than where she was. She's busy all day. She sleeps like a log and goes back out as soon as she's up. She doesn't miss lattes like I do." He winked at Trent.

"Oh, I got one of them fancy coffee machines. I haven't even taken it out of the box. You should unpack it."

He raised an eyebrow. "Are you serious?"

"Uh-huh. I ordered it before the wreck. It's on the floor in the pantry. I can't lift it."

Like that happened.

But, if Trent ordered it, he must also like a good espresso. "I will totally set it up. And then I will make up exceptional coffee while it storms later." He felt himself smile. He was kind of excited about the idea.

"Yeah? Excellent. I got good whole-bean coffee in the freezer. A fan sent it from Seattle." Trent was relaxing now, and that angry redness was beginning to fade.

"You have fans? How cool is that? I'm staying with a celebrity."

Trent winced. "Nah, that was before you came here. I'm a bull rider. Rope's a champion."

"Oh, I know all about him. He has quite a story. Jude likes to tell it a lot." He leaned toward Trent. "A *lot*."

Trent's teeth sank into his bottom lip as he tried to fight his laughter. "Oh, lord have mercy, isn't that the truth?"

"When they first moved down here it was every—single—phone call." It was true, but he was also teasing. Jude was proud of Rope; it was part of what made them such a great couple. They were proud of each other. That didn't stop him from giggling though.

"Oh, champ..." Trent did an *amazing* Jude impersonation.

"Now, darlin'..." His version of Rope was pathetically bad by contrast, and Fox rolled his eyes as he started to laugh. "Wow."

Trent howled with laughter, the sound near hysterical. "That was terrible! Do it again!"

"Ha! Not on your life, asshole." He tapped the butt end of his beer bottle on the railing, sucking in a breath.

Trent's laughter rolled from him, bubbling out, and the brace started moving under Trent's arm.

"Whoop!" He reached for the brace, catching it before it slipped, and tried to calm his giggles. "That would be bad. Let's get this back where it belongs."

"Yeah. Yeah. I'm so close to getting better." Trent helped him get things back to rights. "I'm not messing up now."

"No way. Not when you have Nurse Foxingale here to help you on a regular basis. Soon with added espresso!" He actually got enough sleep here that espresso was like a treat more than a necessity.

"Oh. Oh, hello, nurse!" Trent's gaze dragged over his body like a touch. "Foxingale..."

He swallowed and couldn't have stopped the blush if he'd tried, so he pretended like it wasn't happening. "That's me." His throat had gone dry, so he reached for his beer again.

"Sorry. Sorry, man. I'm not trying to be skeezy. You're just awful pretty."

"No, no. You're not—I'm just—it's fine," he stuttered. He'd been totally unprepared for that kind of frank appraisal, but he definitely didn't hate it. "You're uh, also... very handsome. I just haven't—made a new friend in a long while."

He didn't mean friend. He meant he was practically a born-again virgin. As if that wasn't even more embarrassing.

"Yeah. I been watching the market, but it's been a while since I went all in."

"Good to know." Was it? Now what? They were a couple of single guys who hadn't had sex in eons, sharing a house. And they'd each just admitted they thought the other was hot.

That wasn't awkward at all.

He checked the strap on Trent's shoulder one more time. "I think I'll go check out that espresso machine. Do you care where I put it on the counter?"

"Nope. Make yourself at home. If you need help... uh... you're fucked?"

He laughed. Again. Trent was really good at making him laugh, putting him at ease. "Also good to know. I will definitely not ask for help."

"You're a brilliant son of a bitch. Have fun. I'll be in after a few."

He gave Trent a nod and escaped to the kitchen, partly to be helpful, but mostly to get away from those eyes, and the way they looked at him. He hadn't moved in to get close enough to hit on the cowboy, but that seemed to be where they were.

The what-ifs mill was fast and furious, so he hurried to the pantry and opened the box.

The damn thing had five million pieces.

He really was fucked.

8

The weather had gone from bad to worse, and their electricity was flickering like mad.

Trent didn't care, but he'd bet Mr. Fox was worrying on his baby girl. Fortunately, they were just next door, and Jude had insisted on a generator, so they'd be good.

Trent stretched out on the lounge chair on the back porch, watching the wind and the rain and the lightning. God was good to him, giving him this show, letting him see how tiny he was in the grand scheme of things.

He thought he'd heard swearing coming from the kitchen earlier. A minute or two later, he'd heard music, possibly to cover the swearing, and then just a bit ago, he was pretty sure he'd heard coffee grinding. He wasn't sure whether Fox just liked to keep his hands busy or if the man had been making an escape when he offered to set up the coffee maker, but either way, they were having lattes. Or cappuccino. Or something.

The damn machine had cost the earth, but he'd got it partially as a joke, because Jude missed his fancy coffees, but mostly because Trent had been known to spend all his daily calories at the coffee shop when he was on the road.

His phone rang, and he knew who it was. Only one person would be calling to check up on him in a run-of-the-mill Texas thunderstorm, and it wasn't a cowboy.

"I'm fine, Jude. How are you, buddy?" He couldn't help his smile.

"How about that lightning, huh? Are you guys good? Is Fox freaking out?" Trent supposed it was a legitimate question. Rope had told him that Jude held his hand through his first big Texas storm.

"He's bashing the fancy coffeemaker into submission. Then I promise to hold him for the storm." God, Jude was adorable. "How's little bit?"

"Which one? They're fine. It's a sleepover. They all scream every time the thunder rolls. Rope is making popcorn. I'm glad Fox is making himself useful. That's what he is there for, right?"

"Yeah. He's a huge help. He brought me a hamburger and onion rings. I like talking to him. He's cool." Fox soothed his soul and tickled his fancy—both things were good.

"He's a good guy. He's just kind of rudderless after a pretty major meltdown. It's good he got away."

"Yeah." He didn't want to hear about it from Jude. He wanted Fox to tell him what the man needed him to know. It was the fair thing to do. "He doctored my shoulder and didn't barf."

Jude chuckled. "He's a keeper then. There's a reason I felt like I shouldn't even try. Rope is better at that stuff."

"Rope doctors critters and little boys that fall off fences..."

"He does. Listen, tell Fox that Amelia is doing great.

She's totally in her element. We'll bring her back in the morning."

"We'll be here with bells on. You enjoy your popcorn and the light show."

"Will do. Night, Trent." Jude hung up just as another bolt of lightning split the sky.

"Ooh..." He pondered getting up and checking on Fox. "You're missing one hell of a light show."

"Yeah?" Fox called from inside. "Hang on, I'm on my way." Fox appeared a few minutes later with two mugs. "I believe I have created an acceptable latte."

"I bet it's great." And if it wasn't, he would lie. He had drunk worse, he had no doubt.

"Don't lie to me, now. It's a new machine, and I've decided I'm going to become an expert barista." Fox giggled in that sweet way and handed him a mug. "What else have I got to do? It looks pretty snazzy in your kitchen, by the way."

"Yeah? Excellent. You like it?" He sipped the latte, finding it pretty darn good.

"I do. It was a bear to set up, but I figured it out." Thunder clapped, and Fox ducked reflexively. "Damn. Wow. This is going on all night, you said?"

"Yeah. Come sit? We can shoot the shit." He loved that idea.

Fox snorted as he sat down. "Is that Texan for flirt?"

"No. That would be knocking boots." He wasn't the world's best flirt.

Fox grinned. "I thought that meant fucking, not flirting."

"I'm way better at fucking than flirting, darlin'." He couldn't have stopped his smile if he tried.

"Yeah. Me too." Fox swirled his coffee, then glanced at him. "Me too."

"That is good to know." He sipped his coffee. "Am I going

to offend you if I told you I got wood over you? It was the first time since the wreck."

Fox blushed again; he could see it clearly despite the storm-darkening sky. The man's smile was frank though, not shy. "You're the first person to tell me that since Xan died."

"Yeah? That's a surprise. You're hot as fuck."

Fox shifted in his chair, leaning forward, as more lightning flashed. "I haven't really wanted to until—" Fox's head tilted slightly. "Very recently."

"Well, I want. I'm not sure physically I can yet, but I want." He did like it when someone was straightforward.

"I feel like we could figure something out."

"So long as it's mutual." He held Fox's gaze. "I ain't a greedy lover."

"Oh, I insist." Fox's look turned heated, and there was suddenly a confidence in the set of man's shoulders he hadn't seen before.

Now, how on earth could no one have been all over this hot fucker? Trent didn't get it.

Fox set his coffee down, then reached for his. "Let's see what I can figure out, here." A hot hand landed on his thigh, and the other went for his belt.

"You done this much, out in the wind and the rain?" he drawled, sucking in his belly to let Fox in. He wasn't going to back away. No way.

"Never. Not once. Like literally everything else I've done since I've been here." Fox sank carefully to his knees and got his belt open. "You?"

"No. This is my first." His first time in nature, his first time in his own house, his first time retired...

Fox's fingers found his cock and curled around it. "It'll be a good story then."

His thighs went tight, and he moaned, the sound tearing out of him.

"Easy, Trent." Fox wiggled his cock free of his jeans, head bending over his lap. "Nice and easy."

"I—this is way bigger than nice, darlin'." Was this real? Was this fucking real?

"Mhm." Fox was true to his word, though, and took him in slowly, tongue sliding down his shaft.

The lightning flashed, and he swore that the image of Fox blowing him was burned into his fucking brain. Forever.

Fox took his time but didn't tease, just tasted and savored and licked, easing up every now and then to circle the head of his cock and drive a knowing tongue through his slit. He got a hum of approval as Fox tasted him again, then licked those hungry lips and took him in deep.

"Jesus, darlin'. You're so damn fine. So hot..." He whimpered, the sound embarrassing, but he couldn't help it.

Fox grunted at that and picked up the pace, head bobbing, fingers pressing into his thighs.

His balls drew up, and he grunted, trying to warn Fox that he was fixin' to blow his stack.

Fox gave his thigh a squeeze, then took him in deep and swallowed around him again.

He couldn't have held himself together for love or money. He shot, his toes curling with pleasure as he came, his balls tight up against his body.

"Mmm." Fox took all of him, then licked him gently before letting him go, blue eyes glancing up at him. "Yeah. Bigger than nice."

"Damn..." He licked his lips, eyes on Fox's mouth. "You like to kiss?"

Fox blinked at him and the man's expression went from sexy to confused to something like panic. "I—uh. I like to, but, um, maybe—" Fox swallowed hard, and his eyes were full of worry. "Maybe not... yet?"

Ah, so it was like that. He got it. That's why he asked. Most guys he knew weren't kissers. Kept that line real clear.

He nodded and smiled. "Fair enough. You want a hand?"

Fox's hands were gentle and helped tuck him back into his jeans. "I feel like I've ruined the moment."

"Nothin' ruined here. Not at all." This wasn't a love affair. This was orgasms in the dark. He was a fan.

He'd take damn near any one of them he didn't have to pull out himself.

"Okay." Fox nodded and stood. "I'm definitely wanting."

"Well, come here, and I'll prove that my one hand is smart." He jumped at a wild rumble of thunder, and that made him laugh. "That one got me."

Fox had a hand on his chest and puffed out a breath as he stepped closer, leading with the sizeable bulge under his fly. "Whoo. Me too."

Fox helped him work the button and zipper, for which he was eternally grateful, and then they freed the fat prick that waited for him.

Trent grabbed a hold, making a circle at the base and sliding up, letting his thumb explore veins and nerves all along the way.

Fox shivered and bent over him, bracing a hand on the back of his chair. "Your hand is hot," Fox whispered, as if that were a huge surprise.

"You did that to me. Turned me right on." And now it was his turn to return the favor.

"It's been ages since I did that. I'd forgotten—" Fox groaned and rocked into his hand. "Fuck. I'd forgotten how much I like it."

"Mmm..." How did you forget? That seemed wild, but he

wasn't going to argue. He was going to jack this sweet cock until Fox gave it up.

The thick cock jerked and swelled in his fingers. Fox made a needy sound and exhaled heavily enough that the breath brushed his ear.

"So fuckin' hot, darlin'. You got this. You so got this." He worked, the drops of precome sliding from Fox's cock slicking the way.

"Yeah." Fox's hips jerked, and he held on tight, pumping in time with Fox's heavy breaths. It wasn't long before the arm bracing Fox's weight started to tremble and give, and Fox nodded his head unevenly. "Soon—gonna shoot."

"Come on. Rain's fixin' to hit again. Gonna be amazing."

The lightning flashed again, bright and sharp.

"Yes, fuck—" Fox nodded faster, then grunted and shook, shooting hot spunk over his fist.

"So fine..." Trent eased up, gentling Fox through the aftershocks. So pretty. He did love a post-orgasmic man.

"Th—thank you." Fox took a couple of deep breaths before moving. "I'll uh—I'll get a towel." Fox looked a little drunk, a little relieved, and a little wide-eyed.

"You can just dance in the rain..." he teased, trying to ease the mood. "Again."

"Not a bad idea." Fox zipped up and winked at him, then disappeared inside, returning quickly with a damp kitchen towel. "Let me clean up that good hand."

"Thank you, darlin'. I appreciate it. You are damn pretty when you shoot."

Fox glanced up and caught his eye. "You are too."

Trent knew he was blushing, and he winked. "Mutual admiration society, huh?"

Fox shrugged, grinning gently. "I can think of dumber things."

He cracked up. "I can think of dumber things I've done *today*."

At least ten or twelve, maybe more.

Fox's chuckle turned into a full-out laugh, then thunder struck, startling them both.

After a second of frozen silence, they both started giggling like fools.

9

"We had pizza, and we played hide-and-seek with flashlights, and Uncle Rope has a movie room, and we watched movies and..."

Fox was trying to listen, to stay in the moment with Amelia, who was so happy and excited. He nodded and kept chopping up veggies for his and Trent's omelets.

"Hide-and-seek with flashlights in that storm? That must have been cool."

"*So* cool."

He'd actually woken up thinking he might offer to help Trent get dressed—that was quite a contraption the man had to get himself into—but he wasn't sure he could be alone with Trent again yet. He wasn't certain what they'd done was a good idea.

But if he was honest, he wasn't sure he knew what a good idea was anymore, either.

"Can I have eggs too? I had a waffle at Silas's house, but I'm still hungry."

"Of course, honey. I'll make yours scrambled. Why don't you go brush your teeth and put on some clean clothes?"

"Okay!" Amelia ran off to change.

"Uncle Trent! Did you want to hear about my slumber party?"

He heard a low, soft chuckle. "I sure do, ladybug. I want to hear about every single second."

"Okay. So we went to a movie first, and it was about these bugs that turned into people!"

Trent was great with her. It was adorable. He wondered if it was a funny movie or a scary one. It didn't matter, she'd rarely been this animated and happy, even before they lost Xan.

Trent listened to every word, asking questions, paying attention. Making her feel a thousand feet tall. Fox was grateful for it. For Trent and his friendship. For this whole trip, really. He knew he needed to start thinking about when they needed to get back, but he didn't want to yet.

Eventually, she went to change, and Trent wandered in. "Hey, darlin'. Smells good. She's going to crash so hard..."

He grinned. "Yeah. I'll feed her if she actually makes it back out here, and when she falls over, I'll tuck her in. She had a great time. Did you see that smile?"

"I did. She's very proud of herself. Good deal. She deserves it. You sleep good?"

"Yes." *I dreamed about your handsome face all night.* And he was admiring that handsome face right now, as a matter of fact. "I did. Comfy bed, rain tapping on the window, a little buzz from that orgasm..." He winked at Trent.

It was a little overwhelming; he hadn't had anyone's hand but his in a long time.

"It was fine as frog's hair, yessir." Trent winked at him, and that smile was brilliant. "I think—"

"Daddy! Daddy, I talked to all my friends last night, and they say we can move here!"

Shit. Well, that just moved their travel plans back to the top of his agenda. "Yeah? Well, that was very nice, but all your other friends are in New York, right? What about them? And school?"

"Those are people at school, and there's school here. Just like at home, except that there's Porch Aces and horses and they *like* me."

Just people at school? "What's a Porch Ace?"

"You have animals! And you take them to the fair."

Trent cleared his throat. "4-H."

He raised an eyebrow and bit his lips together so he didn't laugh. Because that would be mean. And he didn't dare even glance at Trent because he knew that would set him off.

"That sound like fun. And a lot of work too, right?"

"Everything's work, right? But you're in a good place to do it. And see how happy Silas is now?"

"Gonna grab a cup of coffee..." Trent didn't look at him, but he was grinning.

Why was it so hard to argue with children? Everything they said was so honest. "Silas does seem happy." But Rope had already had a ranch. He didn't have anything here, and Trent was kind, but he was sure they'd wear out their welcome here if he wasn't careful.

He ignored the voice reminding him that he had plenty of money to buy something if he wanted it, and a place to sell in New York too.

He sighed and tried changing the subject. "Do you want to scramble your own eggs?"

"Sure. I can. I have chickens! Daddy! I can scramble my OWN EGGS!"

Trent's shoulders were shaking good and hard.

"Uncle Trent will let us sublet. We'll be roommates. It will be so fun. We can read to him."

His attempt at a subject change was a spectacular fail. Fox's lips twitched as he tried not to laugh. "You have it all planned out, huh?"

"Well, duh. It's *easy*." She rolled her eyes at him. "It's better here."

He had no idea how to argue because he wasn't convinced she was wrong. "We'll see."

"We'll see always means no." Amelia pouted and scrambled her eggs.

"Not always." But it was pretty much always, she had a point.

"No. That means you aren't going to try hard. I want to try hard to be here and have a new life."

Damn.

Amelia had become so much like Xan. When had that happened?

To his credit, Trent didn't make a sound, but his shoulders weren't shaking anymore either.

"I will try hard to figure out what's next for us. Is that fair? And I hear what you want. Okay? I hear you."

"Thank you." She kissed his cheek. "I will hear what you want, Daddy. We're a set."

He pulled her into a tight hug. He was so proud of her. "When I figure that out, I'll let you know. Salt and pepper, you and me." He winked at her.

"Peanut butter and jelly!" She kissed his cheek. "Jelly jelly jelly!"

She always made him smile. He laughed and let her go. "You all scrambled? Let's get the pan hot."

"Okay, Daddy. I'm scrambled all up." She laughed, shaking her butt, and now Trent did crack up.

He laughed too, and Amelia giggled at them and it felt so good. So real and easy.

He put her eggs in first, and they cooked up fast while Trent made coffee and got her some orange juice. Trent's fridge had some food in it, but he was going to have to make a list and stock it up again this afternoon.

"Did you have a good time yesterday, Uncle Trent?"

Trent nodded, only pinking a little. "We watched the rain and talked."

"There was a lot of thunder. I had a lot of people around so I was okay. I'm glad he was here to keep you company."

Fox grinned as he plated up her eggs. "We sat on the porch and watched the lightning."

"Wow! You weren't scared?"

"No, ma'am. I had your daddy here to keep me safe."

"We kept each other distracted," Fox said, maybe more for Trent than Amelia. He tossed all the veggies he'd chopped up into the hot pan.

"Yep. It was nice to have a friend."

"Would you let us be roommates here until we found a house?"

"Amelia—" He sighed. He wasn't ready for this conversation or for her to be pushing so hard. "Let it go for now, please."

"Okay. Can I have toast too?"

"I think there's bread in the freezer..." Trent didn't look sure.

"I need to shop, but there is bread." He pulled a loaf out of the fridge. "I wasn't sure how you handle bread down here. At home, we just leave it on the counter but..."

"Well, I usually do, unless I'm traveling. Right now, I have a loaf in the freezer, so it doesn't go bad."

"I don't think you'll be traveling any time soon."

"Mm garlic bread. Let's have garlic bread for dinner! And spaghetti. And broccoli."

"And meatballs?"

"Meatballs!"

That was one of their favorites. "Trent? Are you interested in spaghetti?"

"If y'all promise not to tease me as I try to eat the noodles, I am in."

"Oh, Uncle Trent. Teasing is mean."

"Yes, ma'am."

"I usually end up wearing a stain from a meatball or a flappy piece of spaghetti. I won't laugh if you don't."

Although... not laughing had been an easy promise before he came here. Now he wasn't so sure.

"Well, if we all laugh together, it should be—"

"Uncle Trent! Uncle Trent! I know! We can all only use one hand to eat! Then it's all fair."

He gave her a comically wide-eyed look. "But then who —who would cut our meatballs?"

Amelia frowned, then her eyes opened wide. "We stab them with our forks and eat on them!"

He looked at Trent, grinning. "I'm totally game."

"Let's do it!" Trent winked at him, obviously tickled to death. "I am so in, girl."

"One-handed spaghetti night is on the books." He shook his head. "But I'm warning you now, I'm not going to try one-handed steak night."

"I'll let you cut my steak up, darlin'. No worries."

He'd been a lot of things to a lot of people in his time, but he'd never been anyone's *darlin'*.

"Good. We can't have you choking, now."

"Nope. Do you like steak, Miss Amelia?" Butter wouldn't melt in Trent's mouth, but the look he got was wicked.

He snorted and flipped their omelets out onto plates.

"No, it's too chewy." Amelia shrugged. "I like chicken though."

"Yeah. I got chicken in the freezer as well as steak and burgers, hot dogs. All that sort of stuff."

"Yum."

"Breakfast." He set a plate down for Trent and a fork alongside it. "I didn't buy bacon or anything. I'll pick some up today."

"Thank you. Do you like biscuits and gravy? There's a diner in town that makes a great one. I'll treat y'all one morning." Trent picked up the fork and dug in, making the best yummy noises.

"I haven't had them, but I'll try anything."

Amelia raised her fork with her mouth full. "I can make pancakes. Daddy showed me."

Trent's eyes went wide. "You can? Honest? Whoa. I can cook hot dogs on the grill..."

"Well, we won't go hungry, will we?" He dug into his breakfast.

Amelia finished her eggs and slumped back in her chair and yawned. "I have to take care of the kittens."

"They're okay for now. How about a nap?"

"Maybe a little one."

She was going to fall asleep where she sat. He got up and pulled her out of her chair. "Come on, baby. Let's get you to bed."

"Okay, but only for a little while. Okay? Kittens. Chickens. They need me."

"I know. Come on." He winked at Trent. "I'll be right back."

"It's so cool. To have animals that love me. And you love me. And Silas and Uncle Jude and Rope and Trent love me."

"You're a lucky girl, right?" He half-carried her, holding her against his hip as they went to the room she was staying in. "And you had so much fun last night."

"Uh-huh." She yawned as he tucked her in. "Love you."

"I love you, honey. So much." He kissed her forehead and sat with her for a minute while she fell asleep. It didn't take long.

He looked around the room and suddenly he could see it—a fresh coat of yellow paint, her white furniture, her big pink beanbag chair in the corner. For a second, all of that felt very real.

He didn't know why he felt like they should go back, but until he could shake that feeling, he didn't know what to do. Decisions were so hard right now.

Maybe he should just do what Amelia wanted. Maybe she was smarter than he was.

10

"So, talk to me, man! What's going on with Fox? Is he staying? Amelia sure seems to think so."

Trent blinked at Rope, then rolled his eyes. "Dude, you're a nosy bitch."

"We got an hour-long drive to get your stitches out. What the fuck do we have to do but talk?" Rope put the pick-up on cruise. "Are y'all... fixin' to be a thing?"

That he did know the answer to. "Shit no. He's not into me. He just needs a friendly hand once in a while, and I'm not going to turn him down."

If he was totally into Fox, that was on him. He wasn't going to be a bitch about it.

He was good at being into men that weren't into him. He didn't mind.

Much.

Rope arched one eyebrow at him. "Lord, he's a Yankee with a baby... Hell, he's Jude's friend. He don't seem like a hand job friend type."

"I think he's still praying that his man pulls a Jesus or a

Lazarus, you know?" There wasn't a thing he could do about that. "He don't talk about it much."

"You gon' let him stay?"

"I guess? He's nice, and he cooks. Miss Amelia's a sweetheart, and he's good to cast eyes on. He can stay until he needs to do something else." Trent didn't know, and he didn't want to talk about it, either. "You think I can get out of this thing yet, buddy?"

Rope snorted. "Do you plan to listen to the doc this time?"

"Excuse me? You been spending too much time with Jude. I've wrapped you and taped you all to hell." It was a fond tease, a familiar one. He'd put Rope back together a ton of times.

"I have no idea what you're talking about. Champs don't get injured." Rope grinned over. "And you're changing the subject."

"I got no answers. He's not a talker, really. He spends a lot of time sitting outside and watching Amelia play and smiling."

"That's better than sitting and crying, I reckon."

"Yeah. I think he was depressed as all get-out in New York."

"I guess I should let him tell you about New York. But I know he wasn't happy." Rope shrugged. "I don't know why he came here, or why he felt like he wanted to move out of our place, or why he is still here, but it's about something even bigger than his husband I think."

"Yeah? Well, if he tells me, he does. That's not the sort of thing a guy demands to know, right?" Besides, he liked Fox. He didn't want to be an asshole.

"Yep." Rope shifted, stretching his back. "So, he cooks? I

wondered why you looked like you were starting to fit back into your jeans again."

"Shut up. But he does, and he's good. Better than Ensure any day." And one-handed spaghetti night was becoming a thing.

"We offered—" Rope raised a hand before he could protest. "I know, I know. You were fine, you didn't need help, you had everything under control."

Rope coughed, and he was pretty sure he heard "bullshit."

"Be good. Y'all have a brand-new baby. My godgirl. Y'all have a full house." And he knew it.

He wanted to hold that baby for real.

"I'm not going to argue with you. You have Fox and Amelia to help out now. I hear she loves chickens?"

"Between the chickens and the kittens, she's over the moon."

"Have you considered goats?"

He shook his head at Rope. "Nah, but I'm thinking about getting a couple of them miniature horses. If I got a breeding pair, I could sell the babies for a nice profit."

"You don't have your hands—or, *hand*—full with the yaks?" Rope's grin was toothy this time.

"Shut up, man. You know you love our yaks." They were cute as fuck, and they were new. Different. He was into them.

"I do. I do love our yaks. They're going to pay for college. I'm a fucking genius."

"Shit, Silas is going to invent a way to beam horses into space or some shit and pay his own way." They all knew it too. Silas was a brilliant little shit.

"Right? He's scary smart. It's wild that Jude just acts like it's no big thing." Rope glanced at him. "It's a big thing, Trent. You know it is."

Rope's phone rang, and he tapped the display on his dashboard. "Hey, baby."

"Hello. Is Trent getting unstitched?"

"Not yet. We're almost there."

"Bring him over after, and we can have dinner. There's a baby here wanting god-daddy snuggles. I'll tell Fox. Sound good?"

"Yessir. Are you cooking?"

"I am. I'll even have dessert."

"Good deal, baby. See you later."

"Good luck, Trent! Bye." Jude hung up.

"We have supper plans."

He chuckled and nodded. "Fox and Ames will love that. They're missing the pool a little."

"Ames?" Rope chuckled. "If they stay, you'll put in a pool."

"Shit, if they stay, I'll put in a protected bike lane between our houses and a big-assed trampoline." Rope *had* a pool.

Rope nodded, eyes on the road. "You want them to stay! I knew it."

Like it mattered one way or the other what he wanted. He wasn't going anywhere. Fox would stay, or he would go.

He didn't have any say in it.

"I'm just getting through, bud, day by day."

Rope pulled into the parking lot. "Okay. Okay, man. Day by day, it is. Today is about your stitches."

And then dinner with my godbaby Faith. Let's get it done, buddy. I'm ready to be in something softer, swear to God."

They headed in, and he reminded himself to live in the moment, act like the dogs and not think too much.

That got men like him in trouble.

11

Fox reread the online form from Amelia's school in New York and clicked the big red "CONFIRM" button.

And that was that.

Amelia was no longer a student in the New York City school district.

He closed his laptop and stood slowly. It was time to tell Trent. It was ridiculous to be nervous about it, Trent was going to say they were welcome to stay; he knew that. They'd become... good friends. Really good friends.

Really, really, good friends.

He shuffled out toward the barn where he knew he'd find Trent doing something he probably shouldn't be doing, but he couldn't say he would be any better at sitting still or taking it easy or any of the things Trent's doctor had likely told him.

He could hear Trent singing, just loud and off-key as anything. God, that was adorable. Seriously.

He rounded the corner, finding Trent fixing what looked like a little girl's bicycle.

"Whatcha got there?" He stuffed his hands in his pockets as he moved closer.

"Bike for Ames. She was crying in her room this morning because she didn't have one. It's a surprise." Trent offered him a smile. "How's you?"

"She was crying?" How did Trent know that and he didn't? "I guess I've been a little preoccupied today. That's a —that's a great bike."

"Yeah? Good. You can give it to her when she gets home from swimming."

"No, no. You did it. You give it to her. She'll love it." He leaned against a tool bench. "I wanted to talk to you."

"Oh, darlin', you can. Every little person deserves to believe their daddy is magical." Trent winked at him. "Shoot. Tell me all."

"I just pulled the trigger. I took Amelia out of school in New York. I have the paperwork, and I'm going to take her down and enroll her tomorrow. Here. In school with Silas." His hands began to shake, and he shoved them deeper into his pockets.

"Yeah? Cool. I know she'll be excited. You okay?" Trent put down the wrench and headed over to him. "You need a hug, man?"

"A hug?" He took a breath. "I don't know? I think I need someone to tell me I'm doing the right thing."

"Okay. You're doing the right thing." Trent didn't seem to be making fun of him. "Schools here are solid. Silas is happy there."

"We can get out of your hair; we can find our own place..." He didn't really want to, though. Trent's house—the farm, the land—felt like home. And Trent...

He didn't have words for Trent yet.

"It's up to you, for sure, but y'all are welcome here. She thinks of this as home, and I got room and all. Why don't you just stay, let school be the big decision for a bit?"

He nodded, exhaling the breath he'd been holding and locked eyes with Trent. "I don't want to move out."

"All right. Then welcome home. You've got a house key. You tell me what else you need on my end, and I'll get Rope on the bike path."

He blinked at Trent a few times, wondering what the bike path was all about, but he didn't ask. He needed something else right now. "I'll take that hug."

Trent's arms opened, one way wider than the other, folding him in. "You're all right. I got you. You got space here."

"Thank you." He exhaled again, but this time when he took in a new breath, it was the easiest one he'd taken in months. "Thanks, Trent."

"You got it." Trent held him—not tight, but close. The man was solid as a rock.

Close was nice, and Fox didn't rush to let go. "You give a great hug." That was probably a stupid thing to say. He almost laughed at himself.

"Thanks. It feels good to give one, you know? It don't happen much."

"No? Well, we can work on that. I'm a fan." Maybe a little too much of one. His balls were starting to ache. He let Trent go gently, before it was too late to ignore the interest his cock was taking in Trent's strength and all that body heat.

"Me too. You want me to do anything, room-wise for Ames? I can."

That was the reason he didn't want to leave this house. Trent could make him smile so hard he felt like he might cry. The man made Fox's chest ache in a very familiar way.

That thoughtfulness, and the way Trent just naturally took care of people, including him, and especially Amelia.

He swiped at his eyes and shook his head at himself. "I'd love to paint it; would you mind? She likes yellow. And I want to get her bedroom set from New York. I keep seeing all her things in there—imagining it. It's weird." He needed to hire movers, though he didn't need to bring much else in the way of furniture, Trent was pretty well set. "Maybe we'll hit the hardware store on the way back from getting her registered for school. You want to come?"

"Absolutely. We should go have an early supper to celebrate. I'm craving Mexican." Trent squeezed him again, then went back to the bike, lifting it off the workbench. "She just needs a little girl to ride her."

"It looks great. I'm not taking credit though. Her magical Uncle Trent should give it to her." Trent was good to them. Amelia should know how good.

"I just wanted her to feel like she belongs. I'm building a bike path for the kids. And I'll order the trampoline, like I promised Rope."

What was he talking about?

"Did I—Did I miss something? Path? Trampoline?" Why did he feel like he was playing catch-up?

Trent blinked, and then his eyes went wide and he blushed. "Oh, I—So, Rope asked me if I was going to put in a pool for Ames, if y'all decided to come and stay. I told him, no. They had a pool, but I'm willing to put in a safe bike path for the kids between our houses and a real nice trampoline to bounce on here."

He stared for a second, then started to laugh. "I didn't realize so many plans hinged on me making a decision. You and Rope were conspiring, huh?" It felt good actually; it felt like they wanted him to stay.

"When I got my stitches out. We were planning fun things, and a path back and forth that's fenced and safe? That's going to get use for a long time."

"It sounds great. I'll order the trampoline. I can help with the path too. I need something to do, you know?" He could afford a trampoline and a lot of other things if Trent wanted.

"Sounds great." That smile lit up the room. "I love the idea of a path going directly from us to Rope—no road, no pastures. Safe for kids."

"You really like kids, huh?" It was so sweet.

"Cowboys love kids, darlin'. It's part of the makeup." Trent grinned at him and shook his head. "I mean, we deal with them all the time at work, right? Those babies are so excited to see us—them—ride."

"Oh, sure. I didn't think about that. The job I left didn't have space for kids. That was one of the reasons I had to resign." One of several.

"Yeah? Did you like it? I mean, do you miss it?"

"I liked it for a while. I liked the money. I liked being the boss. I liked coming home to my family. But after Xan's accident—I mean, Amelia and I were shocked. We were grieving. Coming home wasn't the same for either of us. And then the market shifted, the company was struggling, and I was working constantly. Amelia was with a nanny or friends all the time, and I hardly saw her. I couldn't fix my family; I couldn't fix work. I went from the guy who had it all together, the boss people looked up to, to this guy who had no idea how to do anything and was taking all the blame for it. Rightfully, that was my job. And I just—"

He blinked at Trent. That was more than he'd intended to say, and a lot more than he'd told anyone but his therapist. "I just broke."

Trent nodded, as if that was completely logical. "I can see that. You had a shift. It's real hard, and I—shit, I *knew* I was going to break eventually. You weren't expecting it."

"Well. I knew something was going to have to change. I knew I was unhappy, that Amelia was unhappy... I just didn't expect to lose my shit. And I don't—I don't trust myself, you know? Moving, changing yet more things, it worries me. I feel like it's right. I do. But I don't trust that I know anything anymore."

"Well, you don't have to. You got folks here that have your back, you got time, and you got space. You can figure things on your own time."

He glanced up, catching Trent's gaze again. "That's what my therapist said. I guess she's worth what I paid her." He grinned a little. He'd much rather be laughing with Trent than being a downer. "I think that path will be a good job for me. I'd like to actually accomplish something again."

"Well, rock on. We'll paint Ames's room, we'll build a path, and we'll make things happen. Did I mention about the mini horses?"

"Uh—no? Are you getting a mini-horse? I was just getting used to the whole yak thing."

"I'm getting a breeding set—two mares and a stallion. One of the mares is a proven producer." Trent was all lit up, and it was sexy as hell.

"Amelia will go bananas over miniature horses."

"I'm going to pick them up over the weekend. Want to come with?"

"Sure. Yes. Sounds like fun. Where are you putting them when they get here?"

"I'm thinking that we'll make a little place in the stables, and then if they become a going thing? We'll build them their own enclosure." Trent rolled the bike out of the workshop.

He followed along, chatting about horses and looking around the property with new eyes. He was going to live here. He'd pitch in, buy some things, build a path, maybe learn to build something even. Contribute. Belong.

He and Amelia would both belong somewhere again.

12

"Uncle Trent? Uncle Trent, do you like this dress? Do you think they'll like me at school? Do you think they'll notice if I don't say y'all?"

Lord have mercy, that little gal could talk when she was worried.

School started tomorrow, and she was just about wired for sound.

"Uncle Trent." Amelia looked at him very seriously. "I made Daddy stay here, so this is *important*."

"Yes, ma'am. This is important." He stopped and looked her over. "I like the way that the blue looks with your eyes. It makes them sparkle."

That earned him an instant smile that reminded him so much of Fox. "Okay. Thank you. I better go hang it up so it's nice for tomorrow." She kissed his cheek and skipped toward her room. "Don't want to get chicken poo on it!"

"Nope. Chicken poop is no one's friend." He chuckled and waved her off into her very yellow bedroom. It really made that room pop.

"Well, you were right," Fox called, tromping up the back steps in his new work boots. "I might not know what the fuck I'm doing, but I managed to clear out that area for the trampoline anyway. We just need to level it. We probably need to call in the professionals for that." Fox was grinning under all that sweat and dust and dirt. "Or at least someone to show me how."

"No problem. Greg can come with his grader. Let me see what all you wrought." He loved to see Fox all sweaty and masculine. Turned him on.

"Sure, one sec." Fox grabbed a beer from his porch fridge and opened it, taking a long swig. "Okay. Come look."

He headed down the steps, admiring the huge spot Fox had cleared away. "Damn, man. You did good! Look at this!"

Oh, that would have taken his poor arm forever.

"Right?" Fox put his hands on his hips, looking over the wide area that was cleared of all the stones and ground cover. "I think I did okay. Is it big enough?"

"I think so, yeah. You know, we could do an in-ground one..." It might be a touch safer.

"Whoa. They make in-ground ones? I've only seen the ones with the nets around them." Fox wiped his brow with his forearm.

"Jude sent me a link. You dig a hole, put the trampoline in, put pads on the edges. It's pretty damn cool." And then they'd have to worry less about all the neighbor kids.

"Cool. Let's do it. I'll find a vendor to put one in. I can dig a hole, but maybe not by myself." Fox sipped his beer.

"Oh, we can do that." He was just going to hire a backhoe, because that was less work.

Less fun than watching Fox learn to work a backhoe, but still...

"I don't think you want me near your house with a backhoe." Fox shook his head and huffed a laugh.

"So, I know we decided to just keep the path mowed..." *We* being Rope, who thought it was a great job for Silas. "What did you decide on fence?"

"Uh. Well, I did some googling, and I don't know much about fencing, but I wanted something that would blend a little, you know? So you feel like you're out in nature, not stuck in a tunnel or something. I was thinking maybe like a galvanized wire mesh? Maybe black so it blends in a bit?" Fox shrugged. "But you would know better than me. I just don't want them getting eaten by anything."

"Yeah. I'm going to run barbed wire about six feet outside the main fence. That will keep the critters out, for the most part. I don't want them hurting themselves when they fall on their bikes." He worried. He'd never had to worry before.

"And then we gate each end, right? I'm going to get myself an ATV like yours so we can leave the trucks here."

Trent was taking Fox truck shopping to distract him while Amelia was in school tomorrow.

Truck shopping, lunch out, and then the feed store. He needed chicken feed and sweet feed, plus dog kibbles.

"Thanks for letting me do all of that. It felt good. It made me feel... useful."

"You are useful. The kids are going to be over the moon." And they were going to be the hit of the county, too.

"They are." Fox rested a hand between his shoulder blades. "How are you feeling today? Did you do your PT?"

Trent breathed out a deep lungful. Damn, that was a fine touch. "Yessir. It's aching today, but I did it. I'm a good dog."

"Good. What do you want for dinner?" Fox turned and started heading back to the porch.

"I took out hamburger meat. Thought we'd have burgers on the grill." It felt a little celebratory, after all.

"Perfect. The cheeseburger girl will be very happy. You're good to her." Fox stepped up onto the porch and finished his beer. "Man, when does the heat let up down here?"

"Thanksgiving." Fall came at Thanksgiving. Winter at Christmas. Spring at Valentine's Day.

"What?" Fox drew the word out, eyes wide. "No. Are you serious? Damn."

"Hottest time of the year is September. We got a good HVAC man, don't worry." He had Dan Simpson on speed dial.

"Well, it can't be worse than New York City in August. And I bet it smells better." Fox winked at him.

"Daddy! Uncle Trent liked the blue dress!" Amelia came busting out of the house and into Fox's arms, then bounced back a step. "Oh, you're smelly."

Fox laughed. "I've been working on the trampoline."

"My trampoline! Eee!" She squealed, dancing him around. "It's going to be the best!"

"You're a little excited about school, huh?" Fox laughed as they spun in a circle. "It's tomorrow. It's weird, right? It's not even September yet."

"I know! And we're going to be so busy! We'll be jumping and swimming, and I have friends already. Uncle Jude told me about Girl Scouts and dance and gymnastics and—" She blinked at Fox. "I have little Muffin and Blueberry and Pumpkin, plus my kitties, and my chickies!"

That little girl did love her miniature horses.

"Uncle Trent has burgers laid out for dinner. Why don't you go make sure your backpack is all set?"

"I think it is, but okay. I'll check!" Amelia hugged Fox

again. "And I love cheeseburgers." She gave him a hug too, on his good side, before disappearing again.

Fox shook his head. "Good grief she is wired for sound."

"It's a huge shift. I don't know what school is like in the City; I know that Silas says it's very new, but he managed just fine." They had figured out how to get Ames on the carpool schedule, no sweat.

"She's pretty outgoing, in case you hadn't noticed. I'm optimistic for her. Kids are probably the same everywhere, really. Just trying to make friends and keep up and pass math. Xan would be proud of her, asking for what she wanted and everything. I'm excited for her."

Trent was too. He loved that she was trying new things, throwing herself into life.

Fox opened the door and looped an arm around his waist to usher him inside. "Show me those burgers, and I'll start up the grill. Are you flipping or am I?"

"Doesn't matter. I got chips, onion dip, and some potato salad. Will she eat those? I think there's corn..."

"Not sure about the potato salad, but I love it. Corn is always good." Sometimes it was like they were an old married couple.

It worked, he guessed.

He was having as much sex as your average married guy, he reckoned...

It wasn't long before the grill was going, and the burgers were on. Amelia helped shuck the corn and get it into the pot, and soon enough they had a regular summer feast going.

"No carpool tomorrow, right? I want to drop Amelia off myself." Fox took a big bite of his burger.

"No. We'll head in together, then car hunt."

Amelia glanced at Fox. "You can drive?"

Fox laughed at her. "You're funny. Did you forget who took you to register for school? It sure wasn't one-armed Uncle Trent."

She fluttered her eyelashes at him. "He's got both arms, and he can drive. Sorta..."

He hooted, tickled shitless. "Yep. I'm a sorta driver. I'm getting better."

"Almost trustworthy." Fox winked at him. "You did a good job on the grill though."

"My cheeseburger is *so good*." Amelia rolled her eyes in cheeseburger heaven.

"Thank you. Mine is too. I like the corn best, though." Kids liked to know about food, he knew.

"It's really fresh. Good stuff." Fox always ate well. He paid attention to his food the way he paid attention to everything else.

Including his family.

Including Trent.

It made him a little breathless sometimes, if he was honest.

He just needed to quit casting eyes and be in the damn moment.

"Early to bed tonight, right, sweetheart?"

Amelia nodded. "Bath, book, bed. Like always on school nights. I remember."

"Are you excited?" Trent was—he was stupidly nervous about her first day. He wanted her to be happy.

He wanted them to stay.

He loved pretending like he had a family.

Amelia nodded. "Yes. Kinda scared too, but Silas said he was also when he started and he did fine."

"Starting something new is scary, I know. You got friends

already, though, and I bet you make a ton more. And you got yourself all ready."

Amelia nodded and pushed her plate away. "I'm full. I'm going to take a bath. Will you both read to me tonight? Please?"

"Sure, we can do that." Fox smiled at her. "Uncle Trent can tuck in one side, and I'll tuck in the other."

"Works for me. I'll take the right side." Trent winked at her, smiling as she took her plate to the sink.

"You guys are so weird. I just need a book." Amelia rolled her eyes. "I will call you when I'm ready."

"Yes, ma'am." He could tell that Fox was trying so hard to hide a smile.

"So. Weird," he teased, as soon as she left the room.

"She meant you." Fox grinned at him.

"Moi?" He fluttered his eyelashes, just being over the top.

Fox giggled at him in that silly way he did and stood. "Well, obviously."

"She's a good kid." He wanted to kiss Fox. Was that weird? It was probably weird.

God, he was getting a headache.

Fox started clearing the table and putting dishes in the dishwasher. "Beer on the porch later? Seems like a nice night."

"Sounds perfect. I'm in." He'd screened in the back porch because Amelia and little Brittany Kileen wanted to camp out there a couple of weeks ago. They'd made it to almost eleven o'clock.

They'd just gotten dinner cleaned up when Amelia called them, and then it was not one book but two before they made a big show out of tucking her in, which made them all laugh.

They said goodnight, and Fox closed the door as they left the room.

"I still can't believe she's starting fifth grade."

"Right? She's at a great age, and I love that she's going to have so much to do." And it was just going to get busier.

"Me too. She was busy in New York, but she seems more excited about it here." Fox brushed past him. "I need that beer."

"Grab me one?" He went to turn on the ceiling fan on the porch and settle in the porch swing.

"Uh-huh." A second later, Fox appeared with two beers and handed him one. "No painkillers today?"

"Nope. Not for two days. I'm sore, but I'm not in distress, you know?" He raised his bottle to click with Fox's. "How you doin', Dad?"

Fox clinked and then sat with him on the swing. "I'm... nervous for her. But good. I'll feel better after tomorrow when I know for sure we made the right choice." Fox glanced at him, giving one of those warm smiles. "I'm pretty sure we did."

"She seems happy. So do you, really." Fox was busy now, painting things, working in the yard, making plans. The man even loved those mini horses.

Fox nodded and took his hand, raising it slowly to look at it, thumb sliding over his knuckles.

His belly tightened at the touch, and his cock threatened to fill.

"I know. I am... happy." Fox kissed his fingers, then flipped his hand over and kissed his wrist.

Oh. Oh, fuck him sideways. His nipples drew up, and he knew he was staring, his lips open, tongue flicking out to wet them.

Fox slid closer on the porch swing, close enough that their thighs were touching. "What about you?"

"I—" He put his beer bottle in the little holder. "I'm over the motherfucking moon, darlin'."

And I want you. Bad.

"Can I have that kiss now? The one I should have let you give me that first time?" Fox's tone was quiet, curious.

"If you're ready, I'm aching to." He searched Fox's eyes. "You're damn fine to me, darlin'."

He brushed their lips together.

Fox caught his jaw and pulled him closer, turning his light touch into something much more.

Stronger.

Hotter.

He groaned and gave into the urge that told him he could have a deep, hard drink from those hungry lips.

Fox was with him, moaning softly as their tongues found each other. If it really had been a while for Fox, he'd never have known it. The man's kiss was confident and capable, knowing and needy.

Oh, fuck him, that felt amazing. He was glad he was sitting down, because his damn head was spinning like he was ten seconds into an eight-second ride.

Fox let go of his fingers, and that hand slid up under his shirt to rest on his abs, burning into his skin. Fox was a solid presence beside him. Even if his head was dizzy, it felt like Fox could hold him steady.

He explored Fox's lips, leaning hard into the firm, warm touch. Trent's free hand slipped up along Fox's arm, then around to the solid muscles of his back.

The swing moved, rocking them and creaking a little as they shifted to get closer, to fit better. "I've been thinking about this."

"Have you? Is it as good as you wanted?" Trent hoped so. He was over the fucking moon.

"No. Better. Way better. In my head, I made a total fool of myself."

"I'm not laughing, darlin'. I'm not laughing one little bit." In fact, he felt serious as a heart attack.

"I appreciate that." Fox grinned, and he could feel it against his lips. "It's been a minute."

"I get that. I have you, though. I got your back."

"You do, and your hand is hot as fuck, man." Fox kissed him again, pressing him into the back of the swing.

They started swaying, and it was heady as hell, the rush of adrenaline shooting up his spine.

Fox's fingers slid across his abs and higher, gliding over one nipple, making it draw up hard. "I know I made you wait. I've just been so unsure about everything. But this was worth waiting for."

"I wasn't gonna push you. I'm no asshole. Important things take time." He knew that. He believed that. "Kiss me again."

"Yes, please." Fox nodded, so focused on him, the kiss making everything around them disappear.

This kiss was deeper, slower, and it totally stole all his focus. He tugged Fox closer, wanting to feel more, to know more about that hard body.

"Yeah." Fox responded with heat and hunger. "We need more."

Could he invite Fox to the bedroom? He wasn't sure. It felt like it might be too much for Fox, and there were still bruises and scars. He'd let Fox drive this. Let Fox take what all he needed.

Fox reached back and pulled his own shirt off, dropping it somewhere on the porch floor. "Can I—will it hurt your shoulder?" Fox's fingers tugged at the hem of his shirt.

"If it don't hurt you to look on it, no." He unsnapped the shirt for Fox to push away.

Fox looked confused for a second, then gave him an indulgent look. "Stop that." Fox slid the shirt off his good side easily, then took his time with his other shoulder. "I saw it before the stitches came out."

"You did. I thought you were going to lose it. I was damn proud." He knew he was a little tore up, but all the important bits were there.

Fox chuckled. "Proud of me? For what? Not gagging because your shoulder looked like hamburger?" Fox winked at him. "I wasn't the one in pain."

"Yes." Trent didn't bother to point out that he was always in pain. It was just a matter of degree. "I was damn proud."

"Well, it looks better now. Stronger." Fox's blue eyes flashed. "Sexy."

Thank God Fox liked guys with scars. "I like that."

Those eyes were so goddamn pretty.

"Good." Fox dropped his shirt, so it disappeared wherever Fox's had gone, then smoothed warm hands over his skin. "Mmm. Look at these abs."

He rolled them, showing off some, letting himself feel a little sexy, a little hot. He wasn't pretty as some, but he had the bull rider abs.

Fox slid those fingers over his beltline and cupped his cock through his jeans. His lips opened like Fox had pushed his buttons.

Bingo.

By this point, they knew each other's cocks as well as their own, but almost nothing else. Fox took his hand and placed it in the center of a sturdy, fuzzy chest, giving him permission to touch, then went back to working on his belt and fly with practiced ease.

He dragged his fingers over Fox's skin, exploring the way the planes and valleys moved, seeking out all the hot spots, the sensitive areas. He loved hearing the little gasps, feeling the goosebumps that rose up when he found a good spot.

Fox's foot slipped, and the swing rocked forward, making them both lean into the cushions. When it rocked back, Fox stood and lifted him right up before stepping clear of it with a chuckle. "Damn thing is dangerous." Another shift, and Trent's back was against the wall of the house, and Fox picked up where they'd left off.

Trent pushed up as he leaned down, meeting him halfway. He forgot, most of the time, how much shorter he was than Fox.

The man simply seemed large.

"Gonna have to get you a milk crate." Fox grinned and kissed him again, bracing an arm on the wall and bending a little more so he didn't have to stretch so tall.

"Shut up." He grinned, though, then set to proving exactly how hot a shorter guy could be...

"Oh. Fuck." Fox grunted as he tugged those dusty jeans open and wiggled them low on Fox's hips.

"Mmm..." Trent grunted at the blistering touch of that cock on his belly, like a brand marking him as Fox's. "More."

"More?" Fox rolled his nipple between thumb and forefinger.

"Uh—uh-huh." Damn, that blew his mind, and electricity slammed through him.

Fox rocked into him, cock sliding across his abs. "Yeah. More."

He found Fox's cock, pressing it harder against him, adding to the friction.

"Oh, shit." Fox groaned. "Really? Okay... fuck." Fox rocked again, eyes crossing.

Really what? He didn't follow, but it didn't matter.

He wanted more.

Trent got plenty as Fox pushed through his hand, cock leaving hot streaks on his skin. "Fuck. Hot."

"Yeah. Come on, darlin'. Show me." He felt hot as fuck.

"Uh-huh. Gonna... Oh, God." Fox humped against him a couple more times and then sprayed Trent's fingers and chest, groaning as he shot.

He panted, his own prick heavy and bobbing, aching for a little attention. It wasn't going to take much. Just a touch, a whisper.

Fox was bent slightly, breathing against his ear, then kissed him hard as fingers pushed his jeans open and dove under his briefs.

He grunted, the sound muffled in their kiss. His eyes went wide, and his head snapped back. Yes. Fuck, yes. So fucking close.

"Look at you. Gorgeous." He managed to get a breath before Fox started stroking him hard and steady. "Take what you need."

"Uhn." That was close to yeah, right?

Of course it was.

His eyes rolled and his spine almost snapped as he shot, his toes curling.

"Yeah. Damn, baby." Fox kissed his chin, his jaw, nuzzled his ear. "Damn."

"Make me dizzy," he confessed. "I swear to God, you make my world spin."

Fox nodded, still catching his breath. "The way you make everything but us just disappear."

"You—" Should he ask? "Want to share a shower? I got a nice one."

Fox didn't freeze up like he had about the kissing question, but it took him a second to answer. "I'd like that."

Oh, thank goodness. "Me too. Come on. We'll clean off and get soapy."

They tucked back in, at least enough that they'd be decent if a certain little girl woke up, and Fox followed him quietly into the house.

Hopefully, he could turn this into a twofer.

A man could wish.

13

The first day of fifth grade had gone... okay. Amelia had come home with lots of stories and a little anxiety, which hadn't surprised Fox, but it hadn't been the "wow" first day he'd been hoping it could have been for her either.

Amelia had definitely felt the newbie vibes at first, but she never seemed unhappy. She kept going back, and it got easier day by day as she met kids and found a favorite teacher and joined the Girl Scouts.

A little more than six weeks in, she was up and ready for the carpool every day, she was chatty and eating well and giving him just about the same amount of sass she always had, so he didn't worry anymore.

Not about Amelia anyway.

The only truly stressful thing now was trying to figure out how to get their things packed and moved. He hung up with the third mover he'd called today and tossed his phone on the kitchen counter with heavy sigh.

"Crap."

He needed to do something else for a while. Maybe Trent had a hole he could dig or something.

He found Trent out in the pasture, fixing part of the fence and talking hard on the phone.

"—mess with me, man. I made you an offer on them, you accepted. I put down the deposit. You get them here, or me and Rope will come out there. I guaran-fucking-tee you don't want that."

Fox believed it.

He wondered what it was going to be this time. Zebras? Maybe hippos?

He reached out and ran a hand over Trent's back, then took the section of fence from Trent and held it in place for him.

Trent blew him a kiss and gave him a grin. "Shit, I might be little, but I will lay your ass out. You have those beasts at Rope's place today before five o'clock, or you'll have trouble at your front door at five oh one."

Trent hung up, then grinned, the expression wicked as fuck. "You hear all that, buddy? You ready to get western with me?" Fox wasn't sure what Rope said in response, but it had Trent chuckling. "Yeah. He'll deliver them. We need a couple guys to unload. Cool. Call me."

Fox shook his head. "What am I unloading? Wildebeest? Wild boar? Can I help get western? I used to box in college."

"Beefalo, and fuck yeah, but it won't come to that. I know this guy. He's more lazy than mean." Trent gave him a once-over. "I can see you boxing. It makes sense."

"Yeah?" He lifted one arm and showed off a bicep, then laughed at himself. "I had a decent hook."

"My superpower is that no one man can hit like a bull does." Trent winked at him. "How's it going?"

The man had a point.

"Ugh. I have moving shit to work out. I needed a distraction so I figured you'd have something I could put muscle into instead of brain."

"Always. I want to fix this fence and start work on Ames's horses' barn, if the weather's holds." Trent mopped his brow. "If it doesn't, then we'll figure something else."

He was so ready to get his hands dirty. "Show me what to do. How's the shoulder?" He'd figure out something for the move. He just needed to sit with it a little longer.

"Stiff and sore, but that's par for the course. Hold that so I can string it. Watch yourself if it snaps."

"Oh. Right, got it." He held on, leaning back a bit in case something snapped and watched Trent work. This had to be easier with two people. "I like my teeth."

"I like them too." Trent tightened the wire, stepping back with a nod. "Better. No one will get out now."

"Awesome." He stepped closer and looked at it, then squinted at the sky. "What's next? You think rain is coming?"

"It's pondering it, or so my bones say. If it does, I'll work in the barns cleaning. Or maybe I'll go through some storage shit."

"Well, just tell me what I can do. We don't have to pick Amelia up for hours."

"And then we've got beefalo coming this evening—four females, a male, and four calves." Trent grinned at him. "I'm hoping that they're successful."

"What do you consider successful?" And where were they going to put them? He didn't really understand just buying up random animals, but it was fun.

"Well, they are big sellers, for meat, but they are not friendly, so Rope and I are going to run them all the way in the back, away from the houses and the horses."

"Do you guys hire someone to butcher or do you do that yourselves or..." He had no idea how that worked.

"We send them to a small processor here in town, and we'll only do that with the males. The cows will stay here, and one or two bulls."

"To make more beefalo." He nodded. That made sense. "We had lots of beefalo where I grew up in New Jersey. Weird-looking things."

"Yeah, but folks pay for them. They're Rope's babies. I love the yaks."

He liked them too. "They're cool. I definitely didn't expect to see anything like that when I decided to get away from the city." He crossed his arms and looked out over Trent's land. It seemed like it went on forever. "I think I have to go back to wrap things up."

"Okay. Do you need me to stay here with Ames? Did you need me to come with you? What?" Trent was always so damn present for him.

He turned his head to look at Trent. "You'd actually come with me?" Could he ask that though? Was that reasonable? It seemed kind of above and beyond the call. Trent had already been so generous.

Trent gave him a confused look. "Sure. I have tons of airline miles. You going to have Ames stay at Jude's?"

"Uh." He rubbed his forehead. "I hadn't thought that far. It didn't occur to me that you'd—that wasn't—yeah. I guess that's what I should do." That would work, they went to the same school, and Jude would get it. "Wow."

"You okay?" Trent always asked him that, like he believed Fox would answer honestly.

"Um. I'm a little—" He took a breath and moved into Trent's space, close enough to make it intimate. "You're very good to me. I don't really know why, so I'm having some trouble processing it. But yes, I'm okay. I think I'm good now, because you—because you're just you."

"Y'all are my people, Fox. I want to be good to you." Simple as that. And that was exactly what Fox meant. What seemed so simple to Trent was a whole world of complicated to him.

He looked down into those green-brown eyes. "I called a few different movers; I just don't trust them to do it without me. But I was dreading doing it on my own, so if you're really—I will take you up on it. It won't be more than a few days. I'll hire people to do most of the packing; it's just everything else."

If Trent asked him right this second what "everything else" was, he wouldn't be able to answer. He didn't even know. But there was more, he just felt it.

"No problem. You can feed me pizza and stuff. I've never been outside of touristy things, you know. Just tell me when you want to go."

"Well, maybe Monday after Amelia goes to school? I'd like to spend the weekend with her and then get this done while she has other things to do. Maybe be home in time to pick her up at school on Thursday. Is that too long for you? I know you have animals to look after and all."

Trent must have some folks to do that though since he used to be gone for the rodeo so much.

"I got a guy I hire to help. He'll come and feed, no worries. Jeremy needs the cash."

He slipped an arm around Trent's side, not caring about the sticky heat and Trent's damp T-shirt. "I don't know what to say. I would never have asked if you hadn't—it feels like a very big favor."

"I have your back." Trent held him, thumb rubbing his hip, nice and slow.

"I guess I'm just re-learning what that feels like." He bent and gave Trent a kiss, just a sweet one to say thank you. "I'm used to me and Amelia against the world."

"Well, now it's you, me, and Ames, fighting the good fight." Trent chuckled softly, jiggling him a little bit. "Hell, it's you, me, Ames, Rope, Jude, Silas, and Faith. You got yourself a village."

"A village." He'd had one once, but after Xan had died, people kind of fell away and he'd realized that *their* friends had really been Xan's friends. He worked a thousand hours a week and didn't have friends. He smiled at Trent. "It's a really good village too."

"Yessir. You need me to take any of your stuff to the cleaners? If I'm traveling, they'll need to do my good shirts and jeans."

"Cleaners? Uh... no. All I have is jeans and stuff. You don't have to get dressed up in good shirts for moving shit." He loved how his jeans and T-shirts smelled when he hung them out to dry here.

"Okay. Still, one decent shirt for a supper won't go amiss, I reckon."

"No, we can have a nice dinner. That would be cool actually." He had a feeling Trent dressed up pretty well. He knew Rope did, and he figured cowboys all had about the same look. Crisp. Starched. Nice hat.

Add Trent's little sideways smile to that, and he'd have himself a snack.

"It would, and if I happen to see a fan in the airport, I'll be presenting myself right."

"Oh." *Oh wow*. He pulled back a little and looked at

Trent a little differently. "You have fans! You know, I didn't think when you told me about the coffee—seeing people in person didn't even occur to me. How cool."

"Well, I'm not Rope, but sometimes, it happens. I been around a few years." Trent's cheeks were bright pink.

He smiled at Trent, teasing a little, but mostly just wanting to see more of that blush. "I've never traveled with a celebrity."

"Ha! No one will blink at me in New York, though."

"You never know. New Yorkers are eclectic. The hat might be a clue."

"Mmm... I'll bring a gimme cap for moving stuff."

He hadn't heard that one before. "Gimme cap? Is that sexier than a hat?"

Trent snorted and swatted him with his ball cap. "This is a gimme cap, darlin'."

"Ow," he complained, grinning. "So, a hat and a weapon. Up where I'm from, they just keep the sun out of your eyes."

"Mmhmm... off my poor head, right? You think I need to go to the barber shop before we go?"

He slipped his fingers through Trent's slightly damp hair and tugged the ends gently. "Yeah, maybe. Me too, probably."

Trent's lips twisted. "Yeah? I sort of like you shaggy. It's nice to hold onto."

Oh God, that made him warm all over. "I'll uh—I'll just get a trim." If Trent liked it longer, he'd wear it longer.

"You're sweet to me. You want me to take you to my guy? I can." Trent's lips brushed his temple.

"Sure." He shivered. It was more than the light rain that had started to fall around them; it was Trent's warm lips on his skin.

"You want to go sit on the back porch and make out like teenagers?"

He chuckled and took Trent's hand. "I can't think of anything I'd rather do right now."

"Me either. The work will wait, and the critters are safe." Trent squeezed his fingers. "Let's go play hooky."

14

Lord, his shoulder wasn't loving flying.

Thank God it was nonstop, Austin to New York, but damn, Trent was tender.

On the way home, he was springing for first class.

"Are you excited, darlin'?" he asked. He was. He was tickled to see what Fox's life was like before.

"I don't know. I love the city. I'm kind of dreading all the moving, but I can't wait to share the rest of it with you." Fox took his hand and gave it a squeeze. "I'm mostly excited. Let's go find our ride."

"Sounds good." Please don't let anyone jostle him hard. "I'll follow you."

Fox put an arm around him and pulled him in front protectively. "This is better." Fox steered him carefully, finding the path with the least commotion. "At least we don't have bags to worry about."

"You know it." He'd stored his extra clothes in Fox's carry-on because Fox had clothes in his apartment still.

"Okay. We're headed out that way." Fox pointed to a trio of revolving doors. "A car is waiting for us."

The doors moved slow and had lots of room for luggage so the two of them fit easily with the single carry-on. Inside the airport, there had been a low hum of crowd noise. Outside was loud. Luggage lined the sidewalk, cars were idling or honking, and people were busily getting in and out.

A man popped out of a shiny black car with dark windows and waved. He looked like something out of a movie in a dark suit, dark tie, and a chauffeur's cap. "Mr. Fox!"

"That's us." Fox steered him in that direction "Hello, Paul."

"Good flight?" Paul opened the back door for them.

"Fine. Long. Paul, this is Trent James." Fox handed off their suitcase.

Paul touched the brim of his cap. "Mr. James. Welcome to New York."

"Lord have mercy. Call me Trent." He held out his hand to shake, a little confused. Folks actually wore those hats? How fucking cool was that?

Paul shook Trent's hand and gave him a nod, then glanced at Fox and put their suitcase in the trunk. "Straight to home, sir?"

"Yes, please." Fox gestured for him to climb in the back seat. "After you. Get comfy; it's a bit of a drive."

"I'm just glad to get out of the plane." He settled back with a pained groan. "I swear to God, darlin'..." He glanced to make sure the driving guy didn't hear him. "I'm going to just bite the bullet and pay for first class for us on the way home."

"We could have done first on the way up, but I was afraid you would think I was being too extravagant. I'll switch the tickets for us. No worries." Fox reached up and gently massaged his shoulder. "Do you need your meds?"

"Maybe. I'll wait and see if it gets worse before I take more." He leaned into the touch, but not too much. It was tender. "Lord, it is busy here, isn't it? Even more than Houston."

"The airport is a little crazy, yeah. We'll take a quieter route to my place and avoid the touristy stuff."

"I'm not bitching. It's cool to watch." He wasn't driving, after all...

Fox chuckled softly and kissed his temple. "Oh, complaining about the traffic is practically an Olympic sport here."

"Mmm... Do you have a gold medal?"

"You're not the only champ in town." Fox waggled his eyebrows suggestively.

"Yeah. I tried, but I did win more than a few events, right?"

"Mhm. A lot more than I did." Fox was solid next to him and seemed to have a comfortable confidence about him. "I thought we'd relax a while and then go out for dinner. I have some paperwork I need to deal with for the movers."

"Sure. I can help do whatever you need me to. I'm good at packing." He'd be good at whatever Fox had to have. "I bet Ames will be excited to see her stuff."

"Oh, she's the reason I'm finally getting this done. She's been asking for it. But you know me. I needed to be sure she was happy and be sure we were staying, and..." Fox shrugged. "I haven't always been like this. I'm kind of hoping —well, small steps."

"So are you unhappy like you are now?" It seemed an important question.

"No. God, no. I didn't mean I was unhappy. I just feel

insecure sometimes. Indecisive. Unsteady. I used to be very sure of myself. I'm just different, not unhappy."

Trent nodded. He got that, bone-deep. "I understand that a little bit. I mean, who I am now? Ain't who I was six months ago, for sure."

Fox nodded. "Yeah, I guess you would, huh? Your whole life has changed too."

"Yeah. Not so much as yours, but... I got a lot to figure out, and fast. I got to make the ranch make money. I got a family to provide for now. I got critters." And he would never ever admit it, but he was a little scared.

"Family." Fox smiled and kissed him lightly. "I think your plans for the ranch will pay off, but I get that it takes a little time. You don't have to worry about providing for us, okay? I'm going to help with all of that. We're fine."

He dared to kiss Fox's knuckles. "I just want you to know I'll never be the guy that leaves you wanting."

"Thank you. But we've got each other now and we're not going to want for anything. We're going to make the ranch spectacular."

They went over a bridge and ended up on a tree-lined highway that followed the river.

"Oh, isn't this pretty. We should plant trees along our driveway."

"That's a great idea. When they get big, it will be like a long country lane." Fox chuckled. "Which I have really only ever seen in movies."

"I'd love that. We could plant peach trees. I do love some peaches." Or maple trees, if they didn't want to grow fruit.

"Who doesn't love peaches?" Fox was always game to try anything, which was a good thing and a bad thing because Trent was always full of ideas.

"Cool. Cool. We'll plant them in the spring." He loved that idea, in fact—rows of peach trees, fresh fruit. Yum.

They turned and the trees receded a bit as they drove into a quieter part of New York than he could remember ever having seen before. The street was fairly wide and lined with eight- or ten-story buildings that seemed residential.

"Ah. We're here." The car stopped, and Fox waited for Paul to come open his door. Warm air rushed in, though not as warm as home.

"Welcome back, sir."

"Thank you, Paul. I'll want you later for dinner."

"Text me when you're ready." Paul extended the handle on the carry-on and handed it to Fox.

"Will do." Fox turned to him. "Ready?"

He was. Sort of. He wanted to see Fox's old life, but he didn't want to, in a weird way. "Absolutely. Let's get to work."

Fox led him up the sidewalk to a long burgundy awning.

An older man in a gray bellman jacket and hat stepped up to greet them. "Mr. Fox. Welcome back."

"Hey, Mike. Thank you."

"Miss Amelia?"

"Not with me this trip, but this is Mr. James."

"Good to meet you." Mike nodded to him, then led them to the door and held it open.

"I've added Mr. James to the guest list for the week."

"Yes, we were expecting him. Thank you."

Fox stepped through the doors and into a narrow lobby with marble floors, a reception desk, and a bank of elevators. He hit a button, and the elevator doors opened right away.

"Pretty!" Lord have mercy. This was a fancy-assed place, wasn't it?

They rode up in the elevator to the tenth floor, which

was also the top floor of the building. "It's nice. It's indulgent, though. I'm putting it on the market as soon as we're on the plane home."

Home. He liked that. "Yeah? If you're staying home and not wanting to be a landlord, it's probably the best thing."

"Ugh. I have no interest in being a landlord. Especially not a New York landlord."

The hall was wide, well-lit, and carpeted, and Fox's door had a polished oak look and was framed by an ornate molding. Fox used a card and then dialed some numbers into a keypad and the door popped open.

Fox grinned at him. "No judging."

"Honey, I'm beginning to think you should have been the one judging." Although he had land. Animals. Trees. A bike trail for the kids. An in-ground trampoline.

Fox had totally traded up.

"God, no. I bought this place with Xan. He wanted a certain way of life, and I was happy to give it to him."

The apartment—though it seemed like a stretch to call it something so simple—was huge. Clean. Minimalist.

Shiny.

It was hard to see the Fox he knew being happy in a place so... white.

"There's a bathroom off the kitchen." Fox pointed.

"Neat." He'd seen Fox's bedroom on the way through the house. It was filled with fun things that he'd found on their weird little adventures. It wasn't plain at all.

"What do you need? Do you want to sit and relax your shoulder? Find your meds? Take a shower?" Fox left the suitcase where it was, eyes on him.

"What do you need from me? Is there somewhere to buy a Coke?" *Can I just explore?* "Should I start packing something?"

"I don't need anything today. I'm taking you out to dinner later—informal—otherwise, I just thought we'd hang out. There are Cokes in the fridge. Feel free to wander around. Amelia's room is down that hall on the left."

"Okay. Thanks." Obviously, Fox needed some time and space, so he grabbed a Coke and took a pill, then went to wander.

"Down that hall" was a lot farther than he expected, and along the walls on his way to Amelia's room were pictures of Fox and a man that had to be Xan by themselves or with baby Amelia at the beach, at the park, in bed, at a birthday party...

Lord, the man had been tall, like Fox. He was damn handsome, though, and he didn't seem like the type who had callused hands.

Amelia's room was the only room he'd seen so far that wasn't white. The walls were the exact yellow Fox had chosen for it at home, and the furniture was girly and expensive looking, but he could see why Amelia loved it. There was a dressing table with a tall mirror and a little tufted seat, a fluffy comforter on the bed, and a line of dolls on her dresser.

He took a picture of it and sent it to Rope, so that they could show her they were here. She'd have to tell him all her stories about her dolls.

Also, he was gonna make her a dollhouse for Christmas. That would be a good project.

"You found it." Fox's fingers ghosted over his lower back. "You can see why she misses it."

"Mmm... I can. Her furniture will look nice in her new room. She'll have the best slumber parties."

"I told her we'd call later when we got settled so we

could hear about school today. Jude says they're swimming right now."

"Oh, good deal. She needs some exercise so she's not missing you too bad." He led them out of the room so he could have a kiss.

"Mm. Is this your plan to keep me from missing her?" Fox smiled down and put an arm over his good shoulder, pulling him closer.

"Is it going to work in the short-term?" He took another kiss before easing up. He felt a little like Fox's husband was looking at them.

"I think it might. We may need to practice a little more though, to be sure." Fox took his hand. "Did you get to the guest room yet?"

"I didn't, no. Is it comfy?" He'd ordered a bed husband from Amazon. It was supposed to be here—either today or tomorrow.

"I don't know, I've never slept there." Fox chuckled. "I hope so."

"Me too." God, this was weird, but it was the way of anything new. Anything at all, but especially if it was important.

"So, the guest room is in here." Fox ducked his head in and then stepped aside so he could look as well. It was neat and basic, almost like a hotel room. "It hasn't been used in a long time."

"It's real nice." He'd slept in a thousand hotel rooms that were worse, for sure.

"It's just a few nights." Fox shrugged and gestured toward a room across the hall. "This is—I'll be sleeping in there."

"All right, darlin'." He hadn't expected different. The

man was still very much in love with his husband. Trent didn't belong in his bed.

And it wasn't like they were sharing back home either.

Fox headed back toward the living room. "Lots of stuff to pack up, but I hired people, and they're coming tomorrow."

"All right. Should I start doing something?" He grabbed their suitcase to put it away. It seemed out of place in this white space.

> **ROPE**
>
> How is it there?

Rope's text made him smile.

> **TRENT**
>
> Very fancy. Like WHOA.

> **ROPE**
>
> Jude says things like "pristine" and "perfect". Fancy words. You ok?

> **TRENT**
>
> Yes. Hurting some. It's weird, being in another man's house.

Weird. It was fucked up.

> **ROPE**
>
> It's Fox. You're fine. Go easy on the packing.

He didn't mean it was weird about Fox. It was Fox and Xan. That was almost another man, altogether.

> **ROPE**
>
> Amelia says she hopes you'll pack her dolls carefully. No pressure, dude. LOL

TRENT

Tell her Uncle Trent is ON IT

Like he wouldn't pay attention.

"Everything okay?" Fox gestured to his phone.

"Rope. I sent him a proof-of-life pic." He showed off the image of Ames's room.

Fox chuckled. "And now you have a pic so you know how to put it back together." Fox looked around the living room. "I have a bunch of kitchen stuff. You want any kitchen stuff?"

"Darlin', I grill out. You are my kitchen person." He didn't even know what kitchen stuff to want.

Fox nodded sheepishly. "Right. I'll keep some and donate the rest. This place is a little different, huh?"

"It's wild. You made a huge shift when you came home. Are—are you disappointed?"

"What? Why?" Fox looked genuinely confused.

"Well, this place is very… very—" How to explain what was in his head. He needed to be clear. "Specific. Like a magazine. Our house is very… not. It's for dogs and cats and kids and thunderstorms."

"*Our* house." Fox took his hand. "Is perfect. This place isn't ours; this is what I'm leaving so I can have animals and thunderstorms and one very happy kid with you."

"I'm glad. I just want to give you what all you need." But this place was like a museum. He was scared to sit anywhere.

"You're uncomfortable." Fox nodded. "I get it. Should we get a hotel? That would be totally fine."

"God, no. There's a perfectly good bed in here for me. No reason to waste the money." He was being a dipshit, that was all.

"If you're sure." Fox leaned down and kissed his cheek. "I'm glad you're here. It's not easy, I know."

"I'm here for you, to help you through a hard thing. I didn't want you to have to face this all alone."

"Thank you. I'm not even sure what I'm facing. We'll just see how it goes. But I'm leaving it here, Trent. Whatever it is, I'm leaving it all in New York."

He gave Fox a long hug, hating that his guy was hurting. "Whatever you need from me, I'm here."

Fox sighed into the hug. "This is it. This is all I need from you."

When they broke it off, Fox added, "And maybe a beer?"

15

Fox lay on his side of the bed, staring up at the stripes on the ceiling where the streetlights seeped through the closed blinds. He was tired, but he couldn't sleep. Maybe it was the streetlights; it was dark in his room on Trent's ranch. Maybe it was because that place was home now, and he liked it that way. Maybe it was because Amelia wasn't here.

Maybe. But it wasn't any of those things. He was restless because he was lying in the bed that he used to share with Xan, and he wasn't thinking about Xan anymore. He had Trent on his mind.

Awkward.

He sat up and slid out of bed. He'd get some water and try to sleep on the couch.

Trent's door was open, the bedside light on. The man had on the cutest little pair of reading glasses, a book in his hand, propped up on the bed husband he'd had sent here.

He hesitated to knock, but if they both weren't sleeping, why not? He tapped lightly on the door. "Hey. Shoulder ache?"

"Little bit. You okay?" Trent smiled at him, the look so warm, so fond. "Can't sleep?"

"Nope. Not a bit." He shrugged. "Not my bed."

Trent pulled the covers back and patted the mattress, the offer clear as crystal. He went into the room and climbed right in beside Trent like it was the most natural thing in the world. As if they'd done this a million times instead of—well, never.

That awkward feeling dissolved just that easily.

"Thank you." Fox leaned back against the headboard. "Love the glasses. What are you reading?"

"It's about a thief named Gideon Crew. It's the third one in the series. Good old mind candy. I got all of them."

"Cool. I haven't read a book in years. I used to read a lot. I loved mysteries, forensic thrillers, things like that. And biographies." He decided he'd pick up a book while they were out tomorrow.

"Yeah? I always have a book in my bag, my truck, and my bedside table."

He was surprised, and he was a little embarrassed that he was, to be honest.

"I love learning new things about you." Like the reading glasses. He grinned over. "You know, I might be more comfortable than that backrest."

"You think? Can I try?" Trent leaned hard, snuggling in close.

"Mhm." He nuzzled Trent's temple. The man smelled like a cowboy, even in New York. "What do you think?"

"I think you smell like heaven." Trent sighed softly, fingers randomly stroking his belly.

"I think you're hitting on me." He tucked his arm tighter around Trent, being careful of that shoulder. It was an easy habit now.

"Would I do that, darlin'?"

Wicked man. It was true though. Trent never made him feel unwanted.

The feeling was mutual. He had to wonder why they hadn't done this sooner—ended up in the same bed. It's not like they were teenagers. "I hope so."

"Oh, good. Can I kiss you? Make you feel good?" Trent waited for his nod before kissing him, nice and slow.

Fucking hell, when Trent kissed him like that it set him right on fire. That slow burn could have him buzzing for hours. He returned the kiss, making sure Trent felt his heat, which was laser focused on Trent's scent, his tight abs, his strength.

His body knew what it wanted, what he needed, and he intended to take it.

Assuming Trent was into it.

He really hoped Trent was into it.

Trent hummed, cock hard as a rock, pushing at the soft shorts he was wearing.

A grin tugged at the corner of his mouth. Trent was into it. He reached up and pulled his shirt off, suddenly very happy that he hadn't been able to sleep. "I wasn't expecting —I mean, I didn't plan—fuck, never mind, who cares?" He helped Trent with his shorts and tossed them away.

"You don't have to plan. I need you." Trent grabbed him, kissing him like he was suddenly on fire for it.

He grunted as he tossed the backrest away and pushed Trent down into the pillows. "Don't let me hurt that shoulder," he growled before moving the kiss to Trent's neck.

"Bring it on. I been aching for you."

He did like to hear that, in that hungry, gravelly tone.

"Fuck, me too." He rocked against Trent, grinding their

hips together. God, that felt so good. It had been too fucking long.

They were cooking with fire, the bedsprings singing—in harmony. Trent grinned against his mouth, and they both chuckled.

He nipped at Trent's chin, enjoying the tight body under him. Something about being so much larger than Trent made him feel powerful. It made him ache.

Trent hooked one leg around him, holding them close together, adding to the friction.

"Close... already, damn." Fox sucked in a breath and shivered. He couldn't remember the last time he needed more than he did right now.

"Mmhmm... gonna smell like you." Trent nipped at his ear, causing a jolt, a tiny pain.

He hissed, and that sting went right to his balls, making him groan. His hips jerked hard, and a second later, it was over, heat spraying between them. He was sure he'd made some wild sound, but all he could hear was the blood rushing and the sound of his heart pounding in his ears.

Trent was still moving underneath him, hips rocking furiously, cock sliding against his now-slick skin. "Fixin' to..."

"Uh-huh," he managed to reply between gulps of air. He leaned a little harder, giving Trent more to feel. "Gimme, babe."

Trent arched, his mouth open, eyes rolling back. Fuck, that was pretty, and Fox wanted to see it—again and again.

"Yeah. So good." He hung there, just watching, taking in the crease in Trent's brow and the flush that rose up from Trent's chest, and he wondered how anyone ever let the cowboy believe he wasn't beautiful. "Look at you."

Trent shuddered and shook, coming down for him, expression one of pure bliss. "Mmm... stay? Please?"

"Yes, please." He slid to Trent's good side, shivering again as the air hit his damp belly. "Are you zonk-out man or a pillow-talk man?"

"I'm a pillow-talk man, I think. It's been a damn long time since I had someone stay."

"Come here." He slipped an arm under Trent so they could snuggle, finally feeling like he was catching his breath. "Definitely been a long time for me too. And it's not why I poked my head in your room, but I'm glad I did. Although this bed..." He chuckled softly.

"It's a sight smaller than mine at home." Trent kissed his chest. "And... you're welcome there, you know? In my bed. At our home."

"I'd like that. Is it weird that invitation gives me goosebumps?"

"No. No, it's not weird. It's big. It's a real thing, a good thing."

He nodded. It was real and good. "I'm getting used to being half of a whole again and I really like it." He pressed his lips to Trent's forehead. "I really like you." It was more than that, but a lot of other big things were happening all at once and he felt like if he said out loud what he was really feeling—as much as he understood it—it might be too much.

"Ditto. Just remember, I got your back. I ain't in for a good time. I'm all in."

"I know. I remember." Trent was so good about making sure of that. "I'm not doing any of this lightly either." Not with Amelia's future at stake.

"No. You're a good daddy, no question, and I wouldn't

hurt that little girl for anything. She's a great light in this dark world."

"I love how you are with her, you know that? I don't think I've said that before, but I do. You're so good to her, and she loves you." Trent was totally hers now.

"I'm glad for that. She is building herself a little web of folks who love her dearly. It's good for her." Trent chuckled softly. "It's good for me too."

He thought so too. "You really like kids, huh?"

Trent wore a goofy grin. "I'm a cowboy. We love kids."

He chuckled. That did seem to be a thing—cowboys and kids. In fact, he thought Trent had mentioned that before. "We need to tell her. About us."

"Okay. You tell me what you think is best, and I'll do it. I'm proud of you, and her, both." No hesitation at all. Just 'okay'.

"I don't know. Let's keep taking about it." It wasn't just about him, but if he was going to share a bed with Trent, Amelia needed to know why.

"Mmhmm. We got a few days to discuss whatever we need to. Right now, we can just talk about normal shit. How much moving sucks. How good supper was."

"It's fancy steak, but it's good. I figured you'd like it, since you can cut your own meat now..." He grinned and waggled his eyebrows.

"Yeah, yeah. It's handy—I can do all sorts of things with that arm now." Trent flicked his hip with one index finger.

He hummed. "Mhm. It was in my best interest to make sure you stay healthy." He shifted a little so he could look into Trent's green eyes. "Which reminds me, no lifting boxes. Zero. None. I don't care if it's a shoe box. I paid people. Let them do it."

Trent blinked at him, then a dull flush crossed his cheeks. "Right. No reinjuring it, huh?"

"No. You're what, eighty percent? Let's keep it that way." He smiled and smoothed his fingers over that pretty blush. "And don't blink at me; even Rope said I should keep an eye on you."

"Rope is a turd, but... man, I hate having to be careful."

For someone like Trent who was tough and liked to work, he'd bet that really was hard. "One day, it'll be better as it's going to get and then you can do what you can do. But until then, I don't want you back in that arm contraption for love or money."

"No, that thing was hellish." Trent still had fading bruises on his ribs from where it dug in. "I'm voting I don't wear it anymore."

They lay there quietly for a bit, listening to each other breathe. Trent shifted, probably because he needed to move that arm fairly often, and Fox took that as an okay to break the silence. "This was a good idea. I should have done this on purpose sooner, I guess, but how do you know when it's time? I don't trust my judgment like I used to. Not with things like this. I'm rusty."

"No darlin', you're Fox." Trent smiled for him. "It's a great idea because you were ready."

"Ha. And you? How long have you been ready?"

"I think I was ready from the first time I saw you, but I'm weird that way."

Oh... that was... "That's not weird. That's really sweet. And very..." Self-aware. Steady. Patient. "You."

"I guess it is. I'm glad you didn't mind it. I tried not to push."

"You didn't push. You pulled." He hummed, enjoying

Trent's gravity. "You were just what I needed—are just what I need."

"Ditto. You make me happy—you and Ames. Y'all give me a reason."

"I like that. We need reasons." He was going to make sure he was always a good reason. "I was at a loss after my retirement, and I chose to leave. I can't imagine being forced to leave something I love."

Trent smiled, and Fox thought it was a little bittersweet. "You know, from the start, that was the only possible end. Bodies aren't meant to ride bulls."

He didn't think brains were meant to work the way his had been either. "No, I guess not. Is there any video of you riding? If I look you up on YouTube, am I going to find you? I don't know why I never thought to do that before now."

"Sure you will. I had a couple-three ninety pointers, and more than one wreck. The last wreck is up on the web, I know."

"Yikes. Well, I'll be watching that tomorrow." He yawned and hunkered down a little lower, then tugged the blankets up. "Mmm. I think it's bedtime, and I don't even care that I haven't showered. We can take one in the morning."

"Mmhmm. Sleep, darlin'. I got you." A soft kiss brushed his jaw. "Good night."

"Goodnight, babe." He tucked Trent close and kissed his forehead. "Close your eyes. I got you too."

16

Trent watched the folks pack things with kid gloves on, yessiring Fox like a boss. He'd never seen such a thing.

He'd found himself a chair that Fox wasn't bringing—and thank God for that, because the fucking thing was uncomfortable as hell—and watched Fox direct shit like a chute boss.

Impressive.

Also, more than a little hot.

They were fixin' to go out and wander, once Fox had decided whatever he needed to. He wanted to see Fox's old life, so that he could understand it for his new family.

Fox stuck bright pink stickers on a stack of boxes by the kitchen, then wandered over to him, grinning. "Comfy?"

"I'm good. You need help? I'll help, darlin'." He just wasn't sure what he was supposed to do.

"You're good. I'm wrapping up. They're going to load the truck soon. I hate that chair." It must be a pretty small truck because Fox was donating almost everything that wasn't Amelia's.

"It's... less than cozy, that's for sure." They had two recliners and a huge comfy couch at home that were covered in pillows and blankets.

"You look sexy sitting in it though." Fox winked at him.

"That's me. Sexy cowboy in a hard chair." Trent flexed for him, winked.

Fox braced his hands on the arms of the chair and leaned over him. "You really need to understand how hot you are."

Oh damn. That was sexual as all get-out, and he found himself getting embarrassingly hard. "Do I now?"

"Yes. Don't laugh it off. You are. You're gorgeous." Fox leaned down even farther and gave him a kiss that was brief but sizzling.

Whoa. He was happy, that was for sure. "You're gonna make me cream my jeans, darlin'," he whispered.

Fox's grin was slow and smug. "I'm sorry?"

"Liar, liar pants afire." He rolled his eyes and grinned. "Good thing I like you, huh."

"Good for me. You ready to get out of here?" Fox pushed off the chair and stood, still all smiles. "Can you walk?"

"Shut up, you." He chuckled, shaking his head, but he stood, not hiding his need. "Where are we headed first?"

"Amelia's old school." Fox took his hand. "We'll see you in Texas, guys. Keep my daughter's things safe, okay?"

"Yes, sir!" It was like a chorus of minions.

"This is the way to pack," Trent admitted. "They've been crazy careful."

"I tipped them very well in advance and promised more if everything arrived on time and in good shape." Fox winked at him. "It's worth it. As you know, Amelia is worried."

"Yes. She told me this morning that she wants a slumber

party for her birthday, and she expects her dolls and her things at the house."

Fox blinked at him. "Oh, shit. Think I should tip them more?"

"Nah. If they get it to the house, then you ought to, right?"

"I know, I'm paranoid though. I just really don't want to disappoint her." Fox stopped and took one more look around the living room. "This is weird."

"Yeah, I bet. Do you want to stay in a hotel for the rest of the trip?" He would so do that for Fox.

Fox paused for another second, then closed the door. "Considering that guest bed creaks like your grandma, that's not a bad idea."

"And it's no fun to be in an emptying-out place. Let's go stay somewhere and pretend we're on vacation." Trent thought this was a great idea.

Fox gave him a smile. "I like it. Do you want super pampered and spoiled, or boutique hole in the wall? I'll make us a reservation anywhere you want."

"Oh, let's do a boutique hole in the wall. Just somewhere with a clean, good mattress and midnight room service." He could handle that.

"I'm on it." Fox started texting as the elevator began to move. "Well, I have a guy who is on it."

"You have a guy? Is he like yours permanently?" Because Trent was going to have to meet him.

"No, no. It's a concierge service. I used to use them for all kinds of things when Amelia and I were here. Last minute childcare, rides out of the city, theater tickets, restaurant reservations, dry cleaning, grocery shopping... that kind of thing."

Fox said all of that like it was a totally normal thing people did.

"Huh." He had Rope and Jude, and they had him. In his world, that was the good ole boy network.

Fox glanced at him and put his phone away. "I know, I know. I'm sure you're trying very hard not to laugh at me."

"Why? You're fancy, you're in a big city. I can get all that same stuff with my neighbors. I'm glad you have all of us now."

"I was fancy. Now, I'm just a guy with money who lives on a ranch." Fox smiled at him and took his hand as they stepped off the elevator. "And I love it."

He held on, squeezing a little, loving this. "You have miniature horses and a bunch of kittens, after all."

"And yaks! Yak? What's the plural?" The air was warm as they left the building, but there was a breeze that felt like fall was coming.

"Yaks. Absolutely. What's Ames going to dress up as for Halloween, do you think?" He'd bought Faith a little Highland cow costume for her first Halloween.

Jude hadn't been super amused.

Fox laughed. "Yeah, I never know until last minute because she changes her mind at least three times. I'm usually scrambling for a costume for her."

"There will be a couple big trunk-or-treats, and there's always someone who does a party. This'll be the first year I'm home for it." He was typically on the road. October was high season for bull riding.

Fox steered them down the sidewalk without rushing, unlike most of the people passing them by. "Sounds like fun. What are you dressing up as?"

"Cowboy." He had all the clothes, the hat, the boots, and a wee cow to carry around.

Fox snorted, then burst out in a big laugh, giggling so hard he had to stop moving. People walking by were staring. Fox didn't care.

Oh, yeah. He was good. He made his lover laugh. So there, grumpy, busy people!

When Fox got it together, he took Trent's hand again, the giggles bubbling out in short little bursts now. "No. Nope."

"No?" He fluttered his eyelashes, teasing madly.

"Maybe we should go as each other." Fox winked at him.

"Ooh... I could go as a pretty-tailed little fox?" He waggled his eyebrows, winked back.

Fox rolled his eyes. "You're impossible. Amusing, but impossible. I could go in an arm brace."

"I have one you could borrow! What a coinky-dink!"

Fox shook his head and laughed again, the sound always so warm and genuine. "That's Amelia's school," he pointed out. "It looks small from the front, but it goes back almost a full block."

"Wow." That was so much different than the sprawling, multi-grade campus that Ames went to now. "That's cool. She's adjusting well to her new school, though."

"She is. This is a great school, but I think she is happier where she is. This place is very competitive, which isn't really her thing."

"She seems like she's settling in. I love to listen to her jabber on."

Fox nodded. "The way she talks, you'd think she always lived there, right?"

He pondered that a second. "I think she was craving a change, and so were you. She took her cues from you. She was willing to start a new life because you let her be brave."

Fox looked at him. "You think so? I don't feel like I did much of anything. I was trying to find my way too."

"I do. You let her know she could look for her way." It probably sounded stupid.

"Maybe." Fox squeezed his hand tighter. "Yeah. Maybe so. I'm glad, if that's the case. Thank you."

He wanted to kiss Fox, but he knew better. "Just the truth."

"She's as happy as she is because of you too, you know. You're always thinking of her."

"She's part of my family. I love her. I love you, but I reckon you guessed that." He couldn't meet Fox's eyes.

Fox caught his chin and lifted his face so he had no choice. "I'm such a coward. I wanted to say that last night, but it just felt like too much. I love the way you just say what's on your mind, just because it's true. I love you too." Fox looked right into his eyes that time.

He'd never have thought—never—that he would tell someone he was in love, and have the emotion returned, in the middle of a busy street in New York City.

Never.

"Funny we had to come all the way up here to admit all of that." Fox kissed him, right out in the open, right in the street with all those people walking by.

His eyes went wide, but he went with it, kissing Fox good and hard. When in Rome, and all that.

When they parted, Fox was flushed and grinning. "Mmm. I heart New York."

Oh, that was cute.

"I think I might too." Trent winked at him. "Show me around, darlin'."

"Cool. From here, we're going for a walk in Central Park."

They wandered, and it was pretty—cooler than back

home, and so many different folks to look at. He was fascinated by all the colors and energy.

"Fox? Fox, is that you?" A man wearing jeans and a black T-shirt so tight Trent could see his pulse hurried over to them.

"Jameson. Wow. Hi." Fox and the hunky guy shook and bro-hugged. "Good to see you. You look amazing."

"Thanks. I'm doing keto, and I hired a new trainer." Jameson glanced at him, eyebrow arching. "Who's this?"

"Oh, sorry. I'm terrible about introductions. This is—" Fox smiled at him and then back at Jameson. "This is my boyfriend, Trent. Trent, this is Jameson, Xan and I used to spend a lot of time with Jameson and his husband Brad."

"Boyfriend? I mean I knew you left your job, but—wow." Jameson looked Trent over like he was from Mars or something.

Trent smiled, nodded, and held out his hand. "Pleased t' meet you."

Jameson shook his hand. "You sound like you're from Texas. What are you doing in New York?"

"Helping Fox here move home to Texas." The 'nosy' was implied.

Jameson's nose wrinkled. "You're moving to Texas? For real?" Trent heard the disdain, but he wasn't sure whether Fox caught it.

"I am. That's where my family is now. We have a great ranch. Amelia loves it."

"You'll be back. Everyone who moves comes back eventually."

"Actually, I hope not. Listen, we have to run. Take care now. Say hi to Brad." Fox took his hand again.

"Yep. You too. Good luck with it."

Fox rolled his eyes as Jameson turned to walk away.

Trent leaned in. "Good luck with it, huh?"

Fox shrugged and leaned back. "We already have all the luck we need."

"Yeah. Poor guy, doesn't know what he's missing." He winked, knowing that Fox knew what he meant. Where he lived wasn't for everyone, but it was for them.

"Damn right. More the fool, him, as they say." And with that, Fox seemed to just leave Jameson and everything he represented behind and changed the subject. They finished their walk past the Natural History Museum and headed into the park. "I love it up here. There's a lake and a castle. You'll see."

"No shit? A castle? How cool is that?" He couldn't imagine. A castle, in a city.

"Well, it's a small castle." Fox winked at him "It is cool though." The path was tree covered and shady, a nice change from the summer sun. It even felt less humid here.

Trent was loving this—walking and talking, just being someone no one but Fox knew for a minute.

"Amelia and I took this walk on the weekends sometimes. She would pretend she was a princess. Wait until we get up there, the view is really neat."

"I bet she has a few more years of pretending left in her. A couple for sure."

"I think so. I hope so. I'm not in a hurry to have a full-on teenager." Fox led him past the castle and Turtle Pond, which it overlooked, around to a path that led uphill to the castle itself. "So, that's the Delacorte Theater; they do Shakespeare in the Park there. And that's the Great Lawn." And everywhere else were views of the city's tall buildings.

"Wow. Have you ever seen Shakespeare? I saw Hamlet in Honolulu once."

"In Honolulu? How cool is that? I've seen lots of

Shakespeare right here. Xan and I went every summer. It's free."

"They do it in Austin too. We can take Amelia, if you want." There was a ton of things to do in Austin, and it was just over an hour's drive.

Not bad at all.

"Yeah? That would be fun. Maybe she'd like a comedy if they're doing one. I've actually always wanted to see Austin." Fox leaned on the wall and looked out over the lake. "So pretty, in the middle of this crazy city."

"It is." Austin had Lake Travis, Town Lake, Lady Bird Lake—they'd have to explore together. "It's gorgeous."

"Field trip!" Fox chuckled. "Cool. Okay. Next up, a stroll in the Ramble."

They hiked for a couple of hours and were hungry by the time they made it back to the apartment to get their things. Fox packed up quickly, and they were gone—Fox didn't even look back as he closed the door.

There was a car waiting for them to take them to their hotel, which was nestled in the middle of a tree-lined block and looked like almost nothing on the outside.

He smiled at the sight. "Look at this. I like it. It seems homey."

"Right? I've never even heard of this place."

They walked inside and there was a young woman sitting at a small, ornate wooden desk. "Mr. Fox and Mr. James?"

"That's us." Fox smiled at her.

"Welcome. Fifth floor. You'll find an open bar and an extensive menu. Call down any time for anything you need." She held the key out to Trent. "Anything at all."

"Thank you, ma'am. You have a nice day." He tipped his

hat and grabbed their bags, at least until Fox grumbled and took them.

"Watch that arm." Fox bent and kissed his temple. "Please." Fox followed him to the elevator. It was just big enough for two people and two suitcases. "It's a good thing you're sm—uh, not as tall as I am."

Small? Him? Nonsense. "Ooh. I'm short, not tiny. Rope? He's itty bitty."

"I corrected myself!" Fox laughed. "You're solid as a rock, babe." The elevator let them out into a vestibule and Fox stepped aside so he could use the key. "I'm excited to see this place."

"Yeah? Why'd you pick it?" He loved how Fox's mind worked.

"Honestly?" Fox grinned at him. "It was the most expensive place my agent found for us. We have one more night in New York together, just us on our own, so I thought we should splurge."

Trent opened the door, tickled as all get-out. It was nice, a little, to be all pampered. "No squeaky bedsprings?"

"Nope. Not going to miss them either." Fox wandered into the entry room to the suite, which had a comfy-looking couch, a TV, and a bar, then poked his head through a doorway to the right. "Whoa. Got any friends in town? The bed is big enough for four."

"Nuh-uh. Not sharing." Trent was sure about that. He wasn't a player. He was a long-term monogamous type. "We'll roll around on it."

"Yeah, not my thing. We can sleep sideways!" Fox laughed and disappeared into the room. "We can dance in the shower. It's huge."

"Mmm..." They could shower together in there for sure. Hell, they could do yoga.

Drowning downward dog.

"Drink?" Fox put an arm around him and pulled him toward the bar. "I wonder if there's music? Grab the menu; we can order room service."

"Hey, make me your favorite." He did love room service. He was sort of a room service connoisseur.

"All right. And you order us food." Fox got behind the small bar and pulled out a bottle of tequila. "Do you like grapefruit?"

"Love it." He opened the menu, and there was just about anything you could want available. Wow. "You want pasta?"

"Love pasta. We don't have that a lot at home." Fox started pouring and shaking and ice clinked into glasses.

"I always think of that as a winter food. Or at least a post-Halloween food."

"Get something with, like, lemon and tomatoes and capers in a wine sauce, with chicken or fish. Totally summer. Trust me."

"Okay. What's a caper? They're sort of like a pickle right?" He searched for that in the pasta section of the menu.

"They're like—I don't know. Very salty peas. I think you'd like them." Speaking of summery, Fox sat a frothy, fruity-looking drink down next to him. "Paloma?"

"God bless you." He grinned and took the glass. "Lemon caper linguine with garlic bread and a Caesar salad?"

"Perfect. Yes? I think it sounds good. And dessert. Don't forget dessert." Fox sat close and looked over his shoulder.

"Mmm... chocolate or berry? Or one of each? Chocolate cake and berry galette? It has a crust..." He liked crust.

"Do it. We can feed bites to each other." Fox's hand tucked into his back pocket.

"Oh, that sounds hot as hell. I like how you think, darlin'." He flexed, tightening his butt cheek.

Fox kissed his neck with lips chilled by his cocktail. "I like how you call me 'darlin'', darlin'."

"Yum..." He took a sip of his drink and sighed at the tart sweetness. "That's nice. I like it."

"I'd kind of forgotten how much I love tequila cocktails in the summer. They're fun to make too." Fox got up and started poking around. "They have to have a Bluetooth speaker or something."

"We going to dance?" He could two-step with the best of them.

Fox nodded. "We're going to try. Aha!" Fox pulled out his phone, and in a minute, they had music going. "Choose your poison. I have Spotify."

"I want to hear your favorite song." He wanted to know things. He guessed Fox's favorite color was blue, he knew his jeans size.

"Huh. Okay." Fox started scrolling on his phone, picked a song and the solo guitar intro played through the speaker. The rich voice and slow groove of Tracy Chapman's "Give Me One Reason" was warm and familiar. Fox set his drink down. "Oldie but goodie."

"Perfect." He opened his arms, making a clear offer. "May I have this dance?"

"You may have all my dances." Fox stepped right in close and slid an arm around him.

"Mmm... I like that." He hummed as their bodies met, his toes curling. "You smell good."

"Really? I don't smell like I've been hiking all over New York on a hot day?"

"No. You smell like you." Fox smelled like musk and wind and rain to him.

"Hmm okay. Maybe later, I'll smell more like you, hm?" Fox didn't seem to know the two-step but danced him around in a circle.

He did love that idea, yes he did. He rested his head on Fox's shoulder, sighing softly.

17

Dinner was simple tonight—loaded baked potatoes and a big salad—one of Amelia's favorites. If Fox was buttering her up a little, who could blame him? They had big news for her, and despite how close she was with Trent, he still wasn't sure at all how she would take it.

He gave Trent's shoulders a quick squeeze. "Who wants ice cream?"

"Me! Me! When is my bed coming, Daddy? And my dolls?" Amelia's eyes were wide, the excitement pouring off her.

"About a week, Ames. And it'll happen well before your birthday."

"I know. You promised." Amelia nodded, a huge smile on her face. So much trust; it made him a little choked up.

"Strawberry all around?" He opened the freezer and took out the half-gallon of strawberry.

"I'll get bowls. Do y'all want spray cream?" Trent swung up out of his chair, moving nice and easy.

"Not for m—"

"Yes, please!"

"I hear a yes!" He laughed, enjoying Amelia's energy. He'd missed it.

"Two spray creams it is! Chocolate syrup?" Trent was having too much fun.

"Ew. No. I am a strawberry purist." Chocolate? Blasphemy.

Amelia rolled her eyes, but she didn't ask for chocolate either.

So there.

"Okay. Sit, sit." Once they'd scooped out big bowls, he waved Trent back over to the table. "We have things to talk about."

Trent sat, his ice cream complete with chocolate, whipped cream, and a cherry on top.

The sundae was a thing of beauty, and also ridiculous. Strawberry was sacred.

"Sitting, Daddy!"

"Okay. So, Uncle Trent and I..." He took a breath. He'd been totally ready for this five minutes ago, and now he was nervous. "I am in love with Uncle Trent."

"I know." She ate a bite of her ice cream. "Can I try a bite of yours with the chocolate?"

"Sure, honey." Trent pushed his bowl over.

He glanced at Trent and then back at Amelia. "You know? How do you know?"

She shrugged. "Silas told me. I mean, I asked him, and he said that it was love at first sight, like Gru and Lucy from *Despicable Me*. I know about love. I read."

He squinted at Trent. "Silas? How is this a thing?"

"I haven't even told Rope, man. Swear to God." Trent shrugged. "The kids are smarter than us."

"You like to spend time with him. You hold his hand

when we watch movies. You make supper, and he washes dishes, and we're a family." She rolled her eyes. "Duh."

He nodded because all of that was true. Amelia was too damn smart, so much smarter than he was at her age. Fox was so proud of her. "Well. Okay. Good. I'm glad you know. We are a family. And I'm going to start sharing Trent's room now, so if you need me at night, that's where I'll be."

Yep. He said that. He got it out. Go him.

"Are you going to have sex?"

He blinked, but it was Trent who answered. "That's really none of your business, honey. What folks do in the privacy of their bedrooms is private."

Thank fucking God for Trent. He was still trying to get past feeling like he was going to throw up. All he could think was he needed to change the subject. "How is your ice cream, kiddo?"

"I like the chocolate okay, but I think we need strawberry syrup for next time."

"You two deserve each other. Heathens." He chuckled and took another bite of his plain strawberry ice cream. He hoped to never hear the word "sex" out of his daughter's lips again as long as he lived.

"What are you going to do with Daddy's old room?"

That was an odd question. "Put it back to the guest room it was before we got here, I guess? Did you have another idea?"

"We could make an art room or a Lego room or a library."

Oh, they could do that. He was sure Trent would be okay with it. "What do you think, Trent? Maybe we could make it all of those things."

"Sure, y'all. We can make it whatever we want. I'm happy

to have it be a fun room." Trent licked chocolate off his spoon. "We can even put in built-in shelves."

"Okay. I expect the two of you to design this amazing room, and then we'll figure out how to build it together." A family project. He liked that idea.

"Nope. Daddy, you have to help too. It's all of us together."

"All of us together. You're right, honey. We'll do it together." He would give her absolutely anything she wanted.

She nodded. "Did you know, Uncle Trent, that Silas's other daddy died too?"

"Yes, ma'am. I did. I never met him, but I hear about him."

"Silas says that it's cool. He said that love wasn't pie, so I can love you too. He loves Uncle Rope."

"He does, and I love you, little girl."

She gave Trent a searching little look. "As much as Faith?"

"What did you just say?" Trent shook his head. "Didn't you just say love is not pie? I love her like a godgirl. I love you like you were my own."

Amelia slid off her chair and threw her arms around Trent. "I know. I'm sorry. It's important, that's all."

"It is. You're important, kiddo. You are a huge light, and I love you." Trent patted her back. "Are we good? You're happy?"

Amelia was a little sniffly when she pulled away, but she was smiling a big, genuine smile. "I am so happy. I love it here, and I love you. And I won't ask private questions anymore either."

"Oh, I bet you do, and I bet I say the same thing." Trent

grinned and winked, pink cheeked. "Ice cream's melting, chica."

"Oops!" Amelia hurried back to her seat. "It's okay. I like it a little gushy."

Fox rolled his eyes dramatically, the laughter just under the surface. "I don't know who you people are, but your ice cream preferences are appalling."

"We're *cowpeople*, Daddy."

Fox snorted and did his best not to outright laugh, but it was a losing battle. He managed not to look at Trent so he could keep it to a giggle, but he already knew he and Trent were going to lose it later. "You are! You are *cowpeople*!" He was getting there, but Amelia? She was practically full-on ranch-raised at this point.

"Yep! Can I go ride my bike now, Daddy?" She opened her eyes wide, as if he knew she wasn't going to try to sneak back over to Jude's to play.

She could sneak, as long as she followed the rules. "Yep. Be back inside by dark."

"I will. Love you, Daddy. I already did my chore chart stuff! Chickens, kittens, eggs, reading, love on the baby horsies."

"You're a good girl." He tugged her over and kissed her cheek. "Have fun. Be careful. I love you."

"Love you! Yay Friday!" She ran out, and Trent slumped back in the dining chair.

"Did I do okay?"

"Did you—? You're amazing." He laughed and grabbed Trent's silly face, kissing him hard.

"Ooh... hey you. You're moving into the bedroom." Trent pinched his ass.

"I am. Tonight. Possibly right now." He stood and started clearing dishes.

"Oooh. We'll have to make room in the closet for your shoes."

"Yes, I have such an extensive shoe collection." Fox laughed again. He liked to laugh; he felt like somehow it was good for the soul. "I swear to God, Trent. I have never laughed as much as I do with you."

"Good, darlin'. I love being able to joke with you." Trent stood and bent to kiss him.

"Mmm." He caught Trent's nape and held him a second longer than Trent had probably intended. "You were cool as a cucumber with that sex question. That was impressive."

Trent smiled against his lips. "I was trying not to panic. I'm glad it worked."

"Oh. I panicked. Straight up tongue-tied. And I really don't need to hear the word 'sex' from Amelia ever again." Trent could handle that stuff. He'd just proven he was good at it.

"No. No, I'd rather not as well..." Trent let his eyes cross.

"You're totally going to be the sex talk dad, sorry. You're better at a straight face than I am." He grabbed a towel as Trent started washing dishes, and Amelia's comment about how that meant they were in love came back to him, making him smile.

"I've just had experience in being in front of the camera a little. I had to not snarl at folks that deserved growling at."

"Oh! I watched some YouTube videos on the plane home. You're amazing. You look fearless and tough. Wow." He could hardly believe that was someone he knew riding eight seconds on a bull. "Sexy."

"I tried real hard and had some great rides. Had some great wrecks too."

"I skipped those." He didn't need to see Trent get hurt.

"I would have liked to." Trent winked at him. "More than once."

He bent and kissed Trent's temple. "Yeah, I bet. I'm glad you're retired. I don't think my heart could take it."

"No. I saw what watching Rope did to Jude—sometimes it turned him on, but the bruises hurt his soul."

"High adrenaline sports are like that, I guess." He left the last few dishes in the drainboard to dry and hung up his towel. "Let's go move me into your room."

"I'm totally in." Trent goosed him. "I'll start with the closet?"

"Great. Are there some free drawers in the dresser? I can bring my undies." He gave Trent a toothy grin.

"There are!" Trent waggled his eyebrows. "Always room for your drawers."

He laughed. They stormed into his room on a mission, grabbing clothing and moving it from his room to Trent's. It didn't take long; he didn't have much. The last round was his stuff from the bathroom he'd been sharing with Amelia, and he looked around at all of her brushes and lotions and girly things and shook his head.

"This I'm not going to miss."

"No? You don't like the glitter?" Trent's eyes were just dancing.

"I think it's more the volume of items and the persistent scent of strawberries." He grabbed his toothbrush.

"Yes, that little girl does like her strawberry smell-good..."

"Grab my razor?" He didn't have much in here at all. "If you have a thing for glitter, the bodywash is heaven."

He managed to say that with a straight face.

"How would you explain the glitter on your face then?"

He batted his eyelashes. "I just want to be beautiful for you, baby."

"Ooh... pretty, pretty." Trent leaned in, voice low. "But I was talking about the glitter from my bodywash around your lips."

"Oh-ho!" Damn, Trent cracked him up. He couldn't help the giggles. He laughed all the way to Trent's room. "Imagine swallowing all that glitter?"

"It might do awful things to the septic tank..." Oh, so *bad*.

"Unicorn poop?" He dropped his things on the bed and grabbed Trent, tugging him in close. "You're a little nuts, you know that?"

"A little? Lord have mercy, I'm close to bat-shit, but I do love you."

"Mhm." He looked around the room, still holding Trent in his arms. "I think this is the longest I've been in your room ever." He'd avoided it mostly. It was awkward. They hadn't really been bedroom lovers before.

"Well, I think you're right..." Trent tilted his head. "You've seen the bathroom, though. It's awful nice."

It was. They'd shared a couple of showers. "You want to show me where to hang my toothbrush?" He kissed Trent quickly and let him go.

"I do. I have a double sink and room for you. Always."

"Like you were waiting for me to come along." He stuck his toothbrush in the holder and set his things down on the counter.

"Hoping. Not waiting. Just hoping." Trent winked at him. "You can't blame a man for praying for someone."

"No one is more surprised than I am that the answer was me. Or happier." He wasn't just sharing a bedroom with

Trent; he was sharing a life. They were sharing a future. He hadn't even dared hope it would happen again for him.

Trent drew him in and went up on his toes, kissing him hard. "Gonna love sleeping with you tonight."

He grinned, warmed from the kiss. "Is it bedtime yet?"

"Nope. We've still got a wee hooligan wandering around outside."

"She's not that wee." He pulled back a little and smiled at Trent and suddenly wondered for the first time ever if he wanted another kid.

"She's amazing. She wants to go into the Halloween stores near Austin to find a costume."

"We talked about a trip to Austin. I'm in. What does she want to be now?" Amelia was known for changing her mind. Often.

"Something from school? I didn't recognize it, but her bestie is going to match."

Tasha was a tiny little brainiac, and she and Amelia were going to simultaneously cure cancer and own a pancake factory.

Or so they claimed.

"Works for me. Are we bringing the bestie to Austin?" Fox asked.

"We can, iff'n you want to. We can have a whole day."

It sounded like fun, and Amelia would probably love to shop with a friend. "Why not? Are you still going as a cowboy?" He dragged Trent out of the bedroom before he decided they should just stay there.

"I think so, yes. Did you want to have a party? We could go to the haunted hayride, but we took Silas last year and got in big trouble…"

"What? You got in trouble?" He led Trent outside to

watch the sunset—one of his favorite things to do from the back porch. "This has to be a story."

They settled, feet up on the porch rail as they rocked. "Well, Jude was out of town, and Rope and me, we took the boy to the haunted hayride. It ended in tears and Silas calling his dad in New York. Me and Rope sat up with him all night, but man, wasn't Jude hot?"

He chuckled. "Amelia has a stronger stomach. I bet she'd love it. Tasha though... I couldn't say. But I think Jude and Rope are having the party."

"Oh, cool. Then we'll just go over and be guests. Are you organizing the food and shit, or do I need to?" Trent leaned against his shoulder.

"I don't know. I'll call Jude tomorrow and ask what we can do." Fox sighed and watched the sky turn colors. "Pretty, huh?"

"Gorgeous. Seriously. This is perfect. You glad to be home?" Trent took a deep, deep breath, let it out.

"I am. I missed it, and I liked that feeling."

"Believe it or not, I understand. I traveled my whole career, so it felt so, so amazing to be home for good."

He put his arm around his lover's shoulders and watched as Amelia ran toward the house, determined to beat the sundown.

Home for good. He liked that too.

18

"Grape jelly meatballs are so a thing." Trent had a whole Crock-Pot of them, in fact. It was his granny's recipe, and they were a huge hit.

"That's gross, Uncle Trent." Amelia had that nine going on forty-five thing happening.

"Are not. Ask Silas. He'll tell you. You going to get dressed here or take your costume over to the house?"

"At the house. I don't want to get all wrinkly."

"I don't know. I'm skeptical, but I've learned I don't know much around here so I'll be trying them. They smell good," Fox said.

One thing Trent had to say about Fox was that he would, in fact, try anything.

"They are good. So, I've packed the beer, the ice, the Sprites. I have the meatballs—what else?" Jude and Rope were over there decorating the hell out of the house, and he was going to help by holding his godgirl.

"I think that's—oh! The marshmallows."

"I'll get them!" Amelia ran off and returned with three bags of them.

"Now we're good." Fox nodded to him and moved ahead of him to open up his truck.

"Perfect." They had a pile of folks coming out to Rope's, including a passel of cowboys who had been at the state finals in Waco, and a couple of guys from the league. It was going to be a great party.

They drove over with their goodies, and there were already cars in the driveway—Rope's mom was in Texas from now until Christmas, leasing her condo out in Orlando, and the parents of some local friends of Silas along with every one of their neighbors were in attendance.

"Looks like a party."

Amelia's eyes were wide.

"Wow. Look at all of this." Fox was almost as wide-eyed as Amelia.

"So many trucks!" Amelia stared out the window. "There's Tasha! And Madison and Kate."

"Yep. You can go on, if it's cool with your daddy. There's gonna be a lot of candy and bobbing for apples, even a hayride." Trent loved this—it wasn't the trick-or-treating of the suburbs, but it was a party out in the sticks, for sure.

"Daddy?" Amelia looked hopeful.

"Of course. Go have fun. Put your costume on."

"Okay!" Amelia was out of the truck as soon as he put it in park. Silas met her in the front yard, and they were gone.

"Come on, darlin'. Let's go be social, shall we?" He leaned over and kissed Fox's cheek. "We can sit in the backyard and rock the baby."

He knew Fox got... nervy in crowds.

Fox reached over and gave his thigh a squeeze. "Yeah, that sounds good. Thanks."

Jude met them at the front steps with hugs. "Hey, guys. Welcome. Happy Halloween!"

"Happy Halloween! I brought meatballs!" He was so proud of that recipe. It was his potluck to go.

Sometimes, he wanted to be fancier than chips and dip.

"Come in, I have a place with a plug for you." Jude led them through the house to Rope's amazing outdoor kitchen and patted a spot on a long table covered in food. "I'll take the marshmallows. I'm hiding desserts in the kitchen for now."

"Like there won't be a million pieces of candy." Trent teased. "Fox wanted s'mores."

Fox actually blushed a little. "Rope likes to grill. Grills call for s'mores."

Jude smiled fondly at Fox, like old friends did. "They absolutely do. Trent, go rescue your girl from Rope."

"I'm on it. I have a godgirl calling my name!" He wandered through the house, giving man hugs and pats and kisses on the way to little Faith.

Fox trailed along behind him, smiling and nodding at people, saying hello when he was introduced, acting like all of this chaos was right up his alley. The man even took finger-food off of trays and ate everything that was offered to him. He seemed relieved though when they found Rope standing on the back patio with baby Faith all wrapped up in his arms.

"We're here to do our godfatherly duty and let you go mingle and deal with hyped-up youngsters." He grinned and took his little Faith, who was dressed as a little fairy and the cuteness hurt his heart. "Have fun!"

Rope chuckled. "Bull. You just want the baby. I know you."

"Can you blame him?" Fox stepped out of Rope's way. "Have fun."

"Come on, darlin'. Let's park it. We can see everything,

but we're out of the crowd a little bit." Trent knew folks would be coming by, but hopefully only in dribs and drabs.

"Sound good." Fox held a chair for him. "She is so cute."

"She's the most beautiful baby I've ever held."

"Are bull riders like Presidents? Have you held a lot of babies?"

"Nope. Not hardly any." What did that matter?

Fox grinned. "So she's the most beautiful—and only baby you've ever held?"

"Maybe the third, but she's still beautiful. She's going to be amazing like Amelia." Trent had no doubt. His girls were amazing.

Fox settled deeper into his chair, gaze focused far off toward the back fields. "Did you ever want one of your own?"

"Never thought about it. That's a harsh disappointment, to know that no one's going to give you a baby."

Fox glanced at him. "You don't know that."

"I don't." But he had, and that took money he didn't have. He wasn't broke, but having a surrogate was pricey.

Fox nodded. "One day. I'd like to one day."

"Yeah? With me?" God, had he just asked that? That was presumptuous as all get-out.

Fox raised an eyebrow, but there was a little sarcastic grin tugging at the corner of his mouth. "Do you still think this is temporary? You're stuck with me, cowboy."

"No. I mean, I hoped it wasn't a little while thing. I want... you know. Forever." Damn, it was hard to say that, but it was true.

Fox rested a hand on his knee. "I think I'm available pretty much forever."

"Oh, well, turns out I am too, so... go team us." Trent leaned over, offering Fox a little, chaste kiss.

Fox kissed him back, and it maybe felt a little less chaste, but it was quick all the same. "We're yours, Trent. Me and Amelia, we're yours now. We're your family. We can make one of those if you want to." Fox pointed to baby Faith. "Yours this time, if you want."

"If we do it together, it'll be mine, no matter the DNA."

"Of course. You just look so happy holding a baby."

"I am." He nuzzled little Faith, and she cooed, that sound echoing inside him.

"Hey, Trent. Who you got there? Is that my granddaughter?" Deidre climbed the steps from the backyard.

"It is." He grinned, taking his hug easily, careful not to jostle Faith. "Hey, lady. Have you met Fox? He's my guy, and Miss Amelia is his little one."

"Oh! I haven't yet." She went right to Fox and gave him a big hug. Fox blinked at him over her shoulder, grinning. "I've heard *so* much."

"Same. It's great to meet you."

"Imagine. Our Trent. I'm so happy for you both."

"Thanks, lady. Did you get to see the bike path?" It went from their ranch, to Rope's, and to the Whiteheads' on the other side, so that no one on the west side of the road had to cross.

"Oh, yes. It's a wonderful morning walk too. I've been exploring. Did you do that all by yourself?"

"Fox and I did half, and once we knew it worked the way we wanted?" Trent chuckled, bumping shoulders with Fox. "It didn't take the six of us any time to finish the other half."

Fox winked back at him. "We got the job done, and it's great for the kids. Amelia sneaks over here all the time."

Diedre pulled up a chair. "She and Silas are good friends. She seems to have settled in well."

"She loves it, and she likes having Silas as a go-between sometimes, I think. It's a big difference, living here and living there." Trent thought Ames was happy, but nothing was perfect, after all. Some things were just hard.

Fox nodded his agreement. "Silas has been great. He did this already and has been able to help Amelia adjust."

"Well, Silas is an amazing grandson. He's going to come out to Florida next summer for a few weeks and explore Disney." Deidre beamed, obviously so pleased by the thought.

"That will be nice for him, spending some time with you down there."

"I'm looking forward to it." Deidre pulled her phone out and looked at it, then stood. "Oh. Jude is looking for me in the kitchen. Very good to meet you, Fox."

"You too. Very nice."

"You be good to my little girl now, Trent." Deidre kissed the top of his head like she was his own mother.

"I will, lady. Promise." He waved at her. "She's amazing."

"Of course she is. She's my granddaughter!" Deidre laughed and disappeared into the house.

"She's a nice—"

"Trent! Dude, you're not wearing a brace for once!"

"Is that a baby?"

"What's wrong now, did you hit your head?"

Fox glanced at him, then back at the approaching cowboys.

Trent winked at Fox, then arched one eyebrow, hiding his smile. "Y'all best be respectful. This here's my Faith. Watch your damn mouths."

"Kiss my hairy butt, old man." Jesse Odell stuck his tongue out at him, while Guillherme Baca came over, smiling at the baby.

"Um bebe tao lindo, sim?"

"She's gorgeous." He knew just enough Portuguese to get in trouble. "Perfeito?"

"Perfeita, sim. Bom. Bom."

Fox stood to greet them, offering a hand to shake. "Hey. I'm Fox."

"I'm Jesse, this here's Guillherme, and Mr. Shy and Stupid is Vic."

Fox shook all around. "Are you... bull riders?"

"Me and Gill are, yeah. Vic's still learning to grow in his pussy-tickler..."

"Language, Jess. There are little ones."

And Jude didn't hold with cussing around them.

"Don't rush a good thing, Vic." Fox gave the kid a wink. "It's good to meet some friends of Trent's."

Jess just kept talking. "So how are things, man? Arm is good?"

"You know it. I'm still stiff, but I'm working out my muscles. I want to throw some loops by next spring." He wasn't going to do pro roping, but he was a cowboy.

"Cool, cool." Jess looked at Fox. "Is this your baby?"

Fox snorted. "No. My daughter is around somewhere, but she's a lot bigger. That's Rope and Jude's daughter."

Jess's eyes went wide. "Rope had a baby?"

"Yep. All by himself." Trent kept a straight himself. "It was a miracle."

Fox just nodded. "I've never seen anything like it."

"Her name is Faith," Vic said from the back of the pack.

Jess twisted around to look at Vic. "What? How do *you* know that?"

Vic shrugged. "I pay attention. I have goals."

"Baby goals?"

"Baby goals. Ranch goals."

"Sounds like Vic's planning to make some money to me." Fox sounded like he approved.

"Vic's balls haven't dropped yet."

"Don't make me kick your ass," Vic snarled, and Trent casually handed the baby to Fox.

He didn't want to have to beat these boys down, but he knew how.

Fox took Faith and stood, picking right up on his vibe and pacing a couple of steps away. "Hey, baby. Aren't you a good girl?" Fox threw him a worried look.

Gill picked up on it too, uncrossing his arms and taking a wide stance.

Jess sighed. "Oh, come on. Can't nobody take a joke no more?"

Vic's cheeks went hot, but he held up his hands. "Sure. Sure. You want a beer, Jess?"

"Totally. Thanks, man. Let's go find the good stuff." Jess held out one hand, and Vic's cheeks went even redder.

Gill rolled his eyes. "Adoro essa estupidez."

Vic took Jess's hand shyly. "You think Rope has Shiner?"

"I bet he does. Come on... baby."

Oh, good lord and butter. He shook his head, but he had to smile.

Gill chuckled and waved, then followed along behind them.

"That was—interesting." Fox snorted.

He shook his head. "Gay cowboy mating call. Hey, bay-bee!"

Damn fools. They needed to chill out and fuck.

Fox raised an eyebrow. "I didn't know gay cowboys were so complicated. I'm glad you didn't make it that difficult."

"You were gay. I was gay. No one had to prove anything,

right? I could just be... yours." There was no ass kicking necessary.

"Good thing because I sure wasn't up to proving anything."

"You did prove yourself. You let me... have a space to fall in love with you." He was being an idiot, because he didn't have all the words.

"You didn't expect anything, it was easy to just... be. With you."

He grinned, shrugged. "That's good. You needed a little easy, some taking care of."

Fox brought Faith back to him and put her in his arms. "Taking care of, huh?"

"Yes. You seemed so damn sad, darlin'. I just wanted to make y'all smile." And to give Fox all he needed.

"Mission accomplished." Fox stroked Faith's cheek before stepping back. "Should we put her down? She's out."

"Yeah. Let me text Rope and see whether he wants her put in her bed or what." He wasn't sure what her daddy would want.

He sent a text over, and Rope appeared like magic.

"I'll take her to our room. I want to be able to hear her if she cries."

Fox took his hand as Rope left. "Did you get your baby fix? Was it good?"

"So good. Did we get a picture of Amelia in her costume? We need one." He wanted to see if she was having fun.

"Oh. No, we need to do that. I haven't even seen her in it yet. I'm hungry, anyway."

"Let's go explore, then. I heard there's brisket and chili both, and I'm hoping to con Ames into a meatball." He knew they were good. He *knew* it.

"I need to try one too."

"Have you been relieved of baby-duty?" Jude headed for a cooler. "Beer? Coke?"

"Beer, please." He took the bottle Jude offered over. "She's sound asleep, so Rope put her down in y'all's room."

Fox took a beer as well. "How's the party going?"

"Great. Amelia looks adorable. She's running around with her friend and some of the boys. Did Jess find you?"

"He did. He's, uh… with Vic." Like biblically.

Jude glanced at him. "Yes. And a hot Brazilian guy I haven't met before."

"Guillherme. He's a stud." Trent glanced over at Fox. "He does three hundred crunches, twice a day. It's ridiculous, but hot? Sure."

"I will never be that ambitious." Fox winked at him. "I've got enough work to keep me busy." Fox loved being outdoors. He would go for a run down their bike path every so often, but mostly, they got their exercise working with the animals or on the house and the barns.

"I said it was pretty, darlin'. I know whose belly I intend to be watching, long-term." He wasn't what anyone would call sexy—he was a plain old cowboy, but he had what it took to make his man hard and happy.

Fox blushed and Jude caught it, chuckling softly. "I'm so happy for you guys. I can't think of two people I was more worried about, and now I don't have to worry about either of you. It's so great. Rope too, he's just over the moon."

"I've got his back. Don't you worry. I will protect him."

Fox glanced at him, still blushing, but this time, the look was curious and kind.

Jude gave Trent a nod. "Thank you."

"I'm okay, you guys. Really, I'm good." Fox took a swig of his beer.

"Let's get our food. I'm craving a bowl of chili, huh?" He grinned at his lover. "With cheese and onions and Fritos."

"I am so in. Thanks for the beer, Jude."

"You know it. Come back for more, later."

Fox nodded and took Trent's hand. "We just might. But first, chili! And we have to find our kid."

"I think she's out in the pasture with the others, trying to scare each other."

"Sounds right up her alley." Fox squeezed his hand. "Whose chili are we having?"

"Momma Canutt. Hers is amazing—not enough to give a man an ulcer, but hot enough that you know it's chili."

"Sounds great. Bring it on." Fox handed him a bowl.

Trent grinned. "We'll have burning kisses."

"We have those already. We might set each other on fire." Fox raised an eyebrow. "I mean—metaphorically, not —you know what I mean."

Trent snorted, tickled as all get-out. "Kaboom, baby?"

"Hell, yeah." Fox grinned at him, then spooned up some chili and tried it. At first, there were yummy noises, but then Fox's eyes went wide as he swallowed. "Mm. Hot. Oh, man. So good though. But *hot*."

Fox took a swig of his beer, but it didn't seem to help.

"Let me get you some milk..." Lord have mercy. He forgot that Texas mild and Yankee mild were different.

"No, no. I got it." Fox took another bite and grinned as he chewed. "It's fine if I just keep eating."

"Add sour cream," Jude suggested. "And cheese. A lot of cheese."

"Mm. Cheese." Fox was a little pink in the face as he added cheese and sour cream. "It's yummy though."

"Yeah. Texans." Jude winked at him, and Trent stuck his

tongue out at Jude, checking first to make sure no kiddos were watching.

"I'll get used to it. I've gotten used to the heat and yak breath. I'm going to be an honorary Texan soon."

"Yak butter on toast!" Trent rolled his eyes. Honestly, yak butter was... ew, but those fancy-assed fine dining restaurants paid top dollar for every ounce.

"They can't think of anything fancier than toast to put it on?"

Jude rolled his eyes. "I swear, Fox, if I never hear the word yak again that would be okay by me."

"Daddy! Uncle Trent! Hide me!" Amelia ducked behind him, and he looked up to see a bunch of kids running in their direction.

Trent stood up as tall as he could, hiding her. Fox moved right in next to him and they made a very effective wall.

"How's your chili?" Fox asked him, casually, as if there were no way this group would figure out Amelia was hiding behind them.

"It's cool. I think I like the meatballs best, though..." He could keep a straight face.

"Oh, those grape jelly meatballs? They're going fast. I hear they're amazing."

One of the kids stopped short and the whole group came to a halt behind him. "Grape jelly meatballs?"

"Yep. Over there in the slow cooker. Have at."

"We have to try that, you guys." The whole group moved away at once.

"Wait." Amelia ducked out from behind them. "That's... they're going to try your meatballs? Hey, wait up!"

"And there she goes." Fox watched her run off. "We didn't get a picture."

"We need one. Especially when she eats one and falls in love."

"Oh. Good idea." Grinning, Fox put his food down, pulled out his phone, and followed behind the kids. "I'm going in."

"What's up?" Rope asked, peeking around his arm.

"They're trying my meatballs." And they were going to love them.

Rope nodded. "Yeah? I can't believe there are any left. Those things are amazing."

It looked like maybe they were daring each other to go first, but all it took was one kid to give everyone a wide-eyed nod and everyone else dug in. He watched as Amelia took a hesitant bite of one, then popped the whole thing into her mouth.

Fox took pictures, but they weren't going to do justice to how he felt when Amelia turned and gave him a huge smile and a thumbs-up.

"It's always that way, isn't it?" Rope asked.

"Yeah. It's just the name that makes them crazy. You say sweet chili sauce meatballs, and it's fine."

"You could just say you brought meatballs and leave it at that, but what fun would that be?" Rope smiled as Amelia and Silas came over.

"Uncle Trent, your weird meatballs are so good."

"Why thank you! I agree." He bowed deep and got a hug and a kiss on the cheek from Ames.

"Silly Uncle. What am I going to do with you?"

"Love me?" he teased.

Ames rolled her eyes. "I meant what *else*!"

"Go play with your friends. If you don't want to watch scary movies, it's cool, right?"

Ames nodded to him. "Right. And I'm not a baby."

"No, ma'am. Your eyes. Your choice. Tell them Uncle Trent said so."

"And you tell Silas Daddy Rope said so too, youngun." Rope's voice was sure, strong.

"I will, Daddy Rope!" Ames smiled and ran after her friends.

"Aren't we all so secure in our masculinity?" Fox barely hid his grin.

Rope rolled his eyes. "Those kids can push, if you give them the room to do it."

"Of course. They're kids. They're supposed to get it all wrong so they can get it right the next time."

"Is that how it works?" He blinked at Fox. That was a neat way of thinking about it.

"I think so. I remember learning every lesson the hard way. That's how I figured out my place, you know?" Fox shrugged.

"Trent never learned his..." Rope teased, and Trent snorted.

"Shut up."

"That's okay. I'll teach him." Fox goosed him.

He clenched his butt cheeks. "I'll make you kiss it better if you bruised me."

Fox shrugged. "I am so in."

"Okay, I'm happy for you both, but I don't need all the TMI. Gross." Jude rolled his eyes and headed back to the buffet.

Trent couldn't stop his shit-eating grin for love or money. "That's one point for me."

Rope grinned. "You'd think he'd never kissed my ass."

That got Fox laughing, and Trent knew where that was

headed. Fox was laughing so hard he actually had to put his beer down so he didn't spill it.

He wanted to cheer and tell the world—that's my guy. He's laughing, he's happy, and he's home.

19

"Looks like rain." Fox squinted out the window, then wandered back to the counter as the coffee finished. "Maybe a stay-in-and-read day? Put on a fire, maybe a movie. Amelia might like that." He leaned over and kissed Trent's neck. "*After* the rest of the chores, of course."

"Mmhmm. My shoulder loves that idea, huh?" Trent smiled for him. "In fact, I'm going to get her out cleaning up the chicken pen a little like she promised."

"Good idea." He took Trent's shoulder in both hands and massaged it. "Sore today?"

"Tender, yeah. Not awful, just tender."

He kept working his fingers in, gently, but enough to loosen up the muscles there. "Maybe a soak later."

"Oh, I can see that, yessir." Trent's eyelids went heavy.

"Mmm. It's a plan." He gave Trent another kiss on his neck and went to pour them coffee. "I should get Amelia moving. She's reading, I'm sure. Did she come grab food already?"

"I didn't see her yet this morning, no."

He put a mug of coffee down in front of Trent. "Okay, I'll

go find her. Drink your coffee." That shoulder was getting better and better, but it seemed like Trent had a weather ache today. He got that in his knee occasionally from an old college soccer injury.

He stopped outside Amelia's door and knocked. "Hey, kiddo. Are you up?"

"Uh-huh. I was playing with the kitties. What's for breakfast?" Amelia opened the door, her bright red nightie covered in cat hair.

He smiled at her. "I can make eggs, and I think there are a couple of leftover waffles I can heat up."

"I like eggs. Can we have the biscuits from the freezer? Can I go outside and ride my bike?"

"Biscuits it is. If you want to ride, you better go quick, so you can get in a ride before the rain comes. Get dressed. I'll start eggs."

"Thanks, Daddy! Make sure you do Uncle Trent's just right." She ran back into her room to grab her jeans.

He snorted and wandered back to the kitchen, heading for the fridge. "I have been advised that I should make your eggs just right."

"Should you, now?" Trent rolled his eyes and sighed.

"I should. And I shall." He grabbed the eggs, milk, salt and pepper, and got to work. "Can you see if you can find those biscuits in the freezer? She asked."

"Ah, she liked that a lot. I bought two bags last time." Trent stood and headed for the freezer, stopping and staring at the window with a frown.

"Bummer about the rain. Amelia wants to ride her bike. I told her she better get moving if she wants to beat the weather."

"No."

The word was deadly serious.

"No? Is it raining already? It's pretty dark to the north. Are we supposed to get thunder?" They had a little history with thunderstorms and the memory of their first crazy rainstorm together always made him smile.

"I want you to get Ames, take her and the kittens into the middle bathroom, grab some couch cushions, and get in the tub. Right now." Trent pulled out his phone. "Go. Now."

"Bath—oh. Shit." He wasn't an idiot; he could do the math. Weirdly green sky, bathtub—that had to mean tornado. He didn't ask questions; it seemed wise to just do exactly as he was told. "Are you coming?"

"When I can. I got to whistle up the dogs and make sure no one's in the barn."

From the speaker, he heard Rope say, "Did you see?"

"Yeah. Going to the barns here. We'll head over there as soon as it's clear."

"Be careful." Fox grabbed Trent's wrist. He wanted to offer to help, but he couldn't leave Amelia, and he knew Trent understood that. "I love you." He squeezed Trent's wrist and hurried toward Amelia's room.

"Hey, Daddy. I'm dressed so I can ride my bike!"

"We can't ride right now, honey, there's a storm coming. Take the kittens and go into the guest bathroom, and I'll meet you there. Go now. Fast, honey, okay?" He needed to grab some couch cushions. "I'll answer all your questions in a minute. I'll be right there."

"The kittens?"

"Yep." He went for light and easy, but he was scared as hell. Trent's face had been serious as a heart attack. He helped her get the kittens and steered her toward the bathroom. "Go on in and wait for me."

He didn't have time for fear; he had Amelia to look after. He ducked into the den and picked up as many cushions as he could carry, and when he got back to the bathroom, he moved Amelia into the tub.

"Sit, honey. Keep the kittens in your lap." He sat with her, but he barely fit and his knees were folded up high. He thought he heard the wind then, but he couldn't be sure what he was exactly. Rain, wind—he hated that he couldn't just see it for himself.

And he hated that Trent was out in it.

That's when the real worry set in, and his heart beat hard in his chest. He felt like he and Amelia were okay, but Trent was out there by himself.

"Daddy, where is Uncle Trent? What's going on?"

Yes, where are you, Trent?

"Uncle Trent will be here soon." He thought he sounded confident, but he couldn't be sure. "It's a bad storm, and it's safest to be away from all the windows. You know how you have to look after your kittens? Well, he has to look after his animals too. And then he'll come in and be safe with us."

"You promise? You promise he's not going to die?" The tears were about to start.

"I promise." What else was he going to say? They absolutely could not lose Trent, so it just wasn't going to happen. He put his arm around Amelia and hugged her closer. "He's going to be here soon. Any minute."

Come on, baby. Hurry it up. We need you.

A sound like a freight train began to wail, and his heart jumped into his throat. Fuck. Fuck, this was bad. This was fucking—

"Opened the windows, brought some water and chocolate and the dogs!" Trent closed the bathroom door and crouched beside the tub, holding the dogs by their leashes. "It'll be over soon, y'all. No stress."

The house was shaking, the sound huge.

"Trent. Thank God." No stress? He put a couch cushion over Amelia's head. "I've got you, honey, and Uncle Trent is here now, see? We're all okay."

He didn't feel okay. That sound was terrible and the way the house was vibrating felt dangerous. He reached out with his free hand and grabbed Trent's arm, probably too hard, but he couldn't help it.

Trent kissed his temple. "It'll be over in a few seconds. Y'all just stay right here with me. Pet your kittens, Ames. And tell them to be easy, hrm?"

"Oh—okay." Amelia had tears streaming down her face, but he wasn't sure if they were more out of fear or relief that Trent was here. Fox understood, he didn't feel as sick to his stomach with Trent in arm's reach.

"You got this, little girl. We're going to be okay. You hear that sound? It's over. You're going to stay in here, and I'm going to go check outside, okay?"

"Should I—" Fox started to ask, but stopped because no, as much as Trent was going to need help, Amelia needed him. "I'll watch the dogs. Be careful."

"I will just peek out and be back. That's it. Fifteen seconds. Start counting, Ames."

"One, one thousand."

"Two, one thousand." He nodded and counted along to distract himself as he unfolded and climbed out of the bathtub, groaning slightly at how stiff he'd been.

Amelia was snuggling her kittens, counting, her voice getting louder so Trent could hear.

He petted the dogs to soothe them a little, and they seemed to settle down some. Then he poked his head out of the bathroom just to see what he could see.

The house was all in one piece, thank goodness, even if the electricity was out.

Trent stood by the window. "Want to see? It's heading off."

"I don't know, do I?" He moved in beside Trent and stood close, soaking up Trent's calm.

There was a funnel cloud, moving away from them across the pastures.

"Ames? Wanna see? If you do, you'd best hurry. It's fading."

And the rain was starting, hard and heavy.

Amelia joined them and stared out the window. "A real tornado." Her voice was awed, but when Fox looked at her, she was pale as a ghost.

"Hey, we're all okay, see? Uncle Trent and me. Your kitties. Even the dogs."

Amelia shook her head. "What about my ponies? Are they okay? Uncle Trent, are they okay?"

"I put them in the garage, baby girl. That's what took me so long." Trent winked at her. "You know I got your back."

"Oh, thank you!" Amelia leaned hard against Trent, arms still full of kittens. "I was so worried about you. Daddy promised you weren't going to die, but I was still worried."

Fox wondered what Trent didn't have time to do because he was busy with those ponies.

"I'm not going anywhere. Did you see how the sky was green, darlin'? That's a sure sign of tornado, and if you ever hear that freight train sound, you get in the bathtub or lay flat in a ditch, if you're outside. You want to be low."

Amelia nodded seriously. "Low. Okay. I will."

His head started to swim. The idea of Amelia being out on her own in something like this made him sick to his stomach. And the thought that Trent could have—

"I—just going—" He broke out in a cold sweat and bolted for the back door, hands shaking, but the sight of the barn—or what was left of the barn—didn't make anything better. He knew what was happening to him, he just couldn't stop it this time. "Oh, fuck." He managed to make it to the edge of the porch before he brought up his breakfast.

"Uncle Trent!"

"It's okay, baby girl. Go grab a washrag and get it wet with cold water for me, all right?"

How was Trent so calm?

"S-sorry. I'm sorry." He leaned on the porch railing and kind of slid to the floor, holding tight to a baluster with one hand.

"Shh... you're okay. The first one's always a little bit of a shock." Trent's hand was solid on his back, sure.

He just shook his head. He didn't know what to say. It wasn't the tornado as much as all the havoc it was causing in his mind, and how it was all so out of his control.

Just like Xan. Xan had been traveling when he died, and there was nothing he could do.

"I can't—I can't—" Fuck, he needed to not talk, he didn't even know what he was trying to say.

"You don't have to. Don't scare the girl, now. Just breathe. I'm going to get you into the bedroom to rest, and I'll take Ames to the garage to talk to her horses."

"Right. Okay." He took a deep breath and swallowed. "Help me up."

"I got the rag, Uncle!"

A cold, wet cloth landed on the back of his neck, shocking the fuck out of him. His eyes flew open wide, and his heart felt like it stopped for a second. "Oh! Oh man. Oh wow." His brain felt scrambled.

"Okay, your daddy needs a dark room and a lie-down. Let's get him moving."

"I'm hungry, Uncle Trent."

"I'll figure something out since the lights are out. You want a PB and J?"

"What if they don't come back on?"

"We'll wander over to Rope's and have a candle party."

"Candle party! Is Silas okay? Are his kittens okay too?"

He heard all the words, but he wasn't processing them well. He wasn't sure he was ready for a candle party, but maybe if he— "I just need a little time."

He let Trent help him up, and somehow, they made it down the hall to the bedroom. "I'm sorry," Fox said again, stupidly.

"I love you. You just breathe. You're okay." Trent eased him into the bathroom to rinse out his mouth. "Go grab him a bottle of water, girlfriend."

"On it, Uncle!"

Once he was done, Trent sat him on the edge of the bed and took off his shoes.

"I can... you should go. Go ahead. I'm okay." He was so far from okay, but he needed to clear his head and calm his nerves and pull himself together.

"I'm going to take Ames outside to the garage so she can see her babies are okay, then I'm going to take her to Jude to hang out. You rest."

Rest. God, he felt like an idiot.

"Yeah. Okay. Tell Amelia I'm fine, and I love her. She was so worried about you."

She was worried. He was panicked.

"Will do. You breathe, darlin'. I got you." Trent kissed his forehead.

He gave Trent a quick nod and watched him go, then thought about the coping skills he'd been so good at before he'd left New York but hadn't had to use one single time since.

Breathing. Grounding. Distraction.

He probably should call his former therapist, but he really didn't want to. He'd wait. He wanted to work this through with Trent.

For now, he'd rest. He put the cloth Amelia had surprised him with in the bathroom sink and crawled into bed, letting his eyes close for a while.

20

Trent had left Amelia with Jude, and he and Rope grabbed two horses and rope and headed out in the steady rain to find critters.

He wasn't sure if he knew what he was supposed to do about Fox losing his shit, but he wasn't sure if it was okay to ask Rope what to do.

It felt a little shitty, but he needed help.

The barns were down at his place, and they'd found some fence down, but it wasn't terrible.

Expensive as fuck, but not terrible.

A giant pain in his butt, but not terrible.

"So, where's Fox? The house looks okay. You didn't lose anything up there, did you? I know he hasn't done this before, but this would go faster with another set of hands."

"Both barns are gone. He's... he freaked out. Puked and went to bed. I'll go fetch him for supper later if he can..." He didn't know what to say. No one got hurt. They probably lost a couple chickens.

"Went to bed with all of this going on?" Rope clucked.

"He's worse than Jude. Even Jude got moving once he knew the kids would be okay."

"I—Maybe he's got a bug." He didn't know. "Maybe I broke him? Do you think I broke him? Is that even a thing?"

Rope and his horse came to a halt to stare at him. "Broke him? What are you talking about?"

"He shorted out. I don't know if I did it right, taking care of him." And honestly, he had shit to worry about now—what if they'd lost one of the yaks? They'd just invested eight thousand a piece for the herd. Then there were the cattle, the horses. The barn. The barns were going to wipe out his savings. He was going to have to come out of retirement maybe.

He'd tried to do this whole 'be gentle with Fox' thing right, but he was worried.

"I don't think you broke him, man. Sounds like the storm did." Rope hopped down, and they got to work on a section of busted fence. "Jude is better at this stuff than I am, but it sounds to me like you took care of him the best you know how, and that has to be good enough, right?"

"Yep. I mean, storms happen. They got to happen in New York, don't they?" He pulled his gloves on and tightened the wire.

"I don't know about twisters, but they have hurricanes and the like. They know when a hurricane is coming, though."

"I guess so... I hope he's going to be okay. Do you think I should put him in a hotel tonight?"

Rope snorted. "You are new at this, huh? No. You don't send your lover to a hotel. Ever. You pull him into *your* bed, into *your* arms, and you ask him what you can do to make it better." Rope cut the wire off where they'd secured it. "And then you listen."

"Okay." With his luck, what Fox would want was to go to a hotel. Jude wasn't super enthused about sleeping without air-conditioning and fans and all.

At least it was early November, so it wasn't too damn hot.

"Amelia seemed okay. How did she do?"

"Good. She was a little scared, but she was focused on the bitty horses." It felt reasonable for a little one.

"That's good. And now she knows what to do. I'm sure Silas is telling how he told us all what to do. Jude was *so* proud of him." Rope rolled his eyes. "They're adorable."

"They learn fast, don't they?" Trent shook his head and sighed. "I don't want him to go back..."

"Hm." Rope frowned. "You think it's that bad? I can't imagine. He loves you more than that city."

"I hope so. I'll go home once we're done, check on him."

"Don't stress it. Just talk to him. Be real. No bullshit." Rope took a step back and looked at their work. "We're unstoppable."

"Uh-huh. We got yaks to find, man. And about thirty head of cattle."

"Right." Rope turned around and looked out over his land, then hauled himself back onto his horse. He pointed into the distance. "Let's start with those two."

"Yeehaw, motherfucker." He winked and spurred the horse on. "Let's bring 'em home."

"I'M GOING to run home, see if the lights are on there." Trent caught Rope's eyes, needing a few minutes alone with Fox before he came back for Ames or brought Fox here or whatever.

The lights were on here, so he imagined they were okay at the house, but he wanted to go over, check on Fox.

Chill out.

Breathe.

Talk to his lover.

"How about we keep Amelia? They can have a sleepover, and I'll make popcorn in the fireplace so they can pretend the lights are still out." Rope nodded to him. "We'll bring her back around tomorrow."

"Ames? Is that cool with you?"

"Totally! Popcorn party!" She wiggled her butt. "Will you feed my kitties?"

"Always." He winked at Rope. "Thanks, buddy."

"You know it. Say hello to Fox for us. I hope he's feeling better."

"Tell Daddy I love him, and he has to do whatever you say so he will feel better tomorrow!" Amelia called after him as he headed out.

"Will do, baby girl. I'll have him call!" He walked over on the bike trail, avoiding the bigger of the mud puddles.

His head was throbbing, and he wasn't sure if he was worried about talking to Fox or not.

Maybe a little...

The porch light greeted him as he wandered up, and he could tell already that Fox had been working. There was a pile of debris that Fox had obviously swept off the front porch at the bottom of the steps.

"Hey, stranger. How goes it? You feeling better?" He put a smile on his face and headed up the back steps. "Ames is hanging with Silas and making popcorn."

"That's good." Fox nodded. "I'm better. I just needed to do something so I—" Fox gestured to the porch.

"Thank you. We managed to find all the yaks and all but

three of the cattle before it got too dark." He went to take a hug.

"Oh, that's good. Great." Fox returned his hug warmly, but he sensed there was still some tension there. "I'm sorry about—thank you for—" Fox sighed. "I know you didn't understand it, but you were great. Thank you."

"I didn't have to understand. I just wanted to help." He kissed Fox's temple. "I love you. Are you okay?"

"I love you. And yes and no. I haven't had a panic attack like that since before I left my job in New York. It takes a little while to shake it off." Now that Fox was talking, he could see that Fox was feeling fragile. Fox was missing that strong set to his shoulders, and something in his eyes seemed far away.

"Well, I'm sorry it happened, but I'm glad you're back on your feet. Wanna come snuggle?"

"Sure. Yeah." Fox leaned the broom he'd been holding up against the wall of the house and took his hand. "Den? We could have a fire."

"We could. It's nice out here tonight, but the wind's chilly."

"I think I'd like to be cozy." They headed inside, Fox following him, hand in hand. "I'm relieved you found all the livestock. I know you and Rope must be breathing easier."

"Yeah. I—That would be hard." He was a little queasy thinking about it, honestly.

He started a small fire, mostly for the mood factor than warmth while Fox went to their little bar in the den and poured them each a glass of wine.

Fox sank into the couch, took one sip, and set the wineglass down on the coffee table, then took his invitation to snuggle seriously and leaned into him. "I used to have episodes like that in New York after I lost Xan, and they got more frequent and worse until I had to quit my job. I felt so out of control. I felt like everything I wanted professionally, things I cared about personally, the people I loved were just slipping through my fingers. I felt like I was on the edge of losing everything all the time. Every day. And everything I tried to do to make it better just made it worse." Fox took his hand. "It wasn't real. Well, losing Xan was real and worrying about Amelia, but most of it was in my head. I just created this whirling confusion where everything was crashing in on me."

Fox took a deep breath and let it out slowly with a soft chuckle. "See? Just talking about that gets my heart rate up, and I'm fine. We're fine. It's not real."

"We are fine. I have to find three cows and rebuild the barns. You're safe here." As safe as anyone could be, anyway.

"I know. I feel safe. I know you love me. I just thought about Amelia being out somewhere alone instead of home and safe with us or losing you out there in the weather, and the next thing I knew I couldn't breathe." Fox took another breath, but this one was normal, easy. "The barns are important. Just make the calls you need to, right away, and we can get that moving."

"Yeah." He was going to have to do that careful. He'd cost out the lumber and all.

"I can give you my miles card if you need to put money down so things can get started right away, and then we can write a check for the balance."

"Oh, darlin'. I'm going to have to—It's not cheap, and I'm..." He wasn't going to say, because he wasn't broke dick. If he rode a few events and got in the money, he could make it up, easy.

"Hey. No worries. I just need to free up some cash.

Actually, I might even have the cash handy. My condo in New York just sold, and I should have that any day."

"I'm talking like thirty thousand, darlin'. That's a fucking fortune." And he'd feel bad, borrowing that much.

Fox turned and looked at him, holding his gaze seriously. "Trent. Let me put this a better way, okay? Listen to me. We have the money. We can pay for our barns."

He searched Fox's eyes. "Yeah? You're sure?"

"I'm very sure. Trent, you can build any barn you want. As fancy as you want. We have money. Real money, I promise. I will show you." Fox smiled at him. "You can even buy more yaks."

He swallowed hard, his heart starting to race. "I just don't want to go back on the road."

"Baby, you can't go back on the road. Not ever. And you'll never have to. We can turn this farm into anything you want. Wait." Fox pulled out his phone and tapped and scrolled until he found what he wanted. "Here. Look. This is what my condo sold for in New York."

The number was big. It had two commas in it.

"And I'm not paying New York taxes anymore either."

"Whoa. I—" He glanced back up at Fox. "I don't bring near that much to our funds, you know that."

It wasn't a question.

Fox took his hand and squeezed his fingers. "You gave me a home. An amazing life. This is just money."

"I love you." He rested their foreheads together. "More than I can say. I'd love you if you had nothing."

"I love you too. We're a team now. What we bring to this family is everything we have; nobody can ask more than that."

He took a soft, gentle kiss, his heart hurting with how full it was. "I'm sorry you were scared today."

Fox smiled at him. "I was. You know, I thought for a minute that I needed to call Claire, but I didn't want to talk to a therapist. I wanted to talk this through with you, and I'm glad I did. I can't promise I won't be scared next time, but I'll know what to expect, and that makes it easier."

"You should have seen Jude the first time. He was an unhappy camper. Ames, though? She rocked it." His brave kiddo.

"She did. I was proud of her. She really did ask me if you were going to die though. It broke my heart a little. But she believed me when I told her no." Fox picked up his wine again and took a sip.

"I had to get those little horses in to safety. They were just out in the pen." And he was a cowboy. Critters first.

"She appreciated that. You are her hero, you know." Fox nodded. "I'm her Daddy, but you're her hero. Uncle Trent to the rescue. So many times."

"I'm just the man who loves her and her daddy more than anything on earth." Simple as that.

"Like I said. Our hero." Fox kissed him, lingering over it a little and staying close.

"Yours." He cupped Fox's ass and squeezed.

Fox set his wine down again. "Where's Amelia again?"

"Staying over at Rope's and having a popcorn party."

"Brilliant." Fox reached up and yanked his own shirt off and tossed it before kissing him again.

Oh, this was a lovely idea. He dragged his fingers down along Fox's spine, letting it burn a little.

"I'll help you find those cows tomorrow. Tonight, everything can just go away." Fox tugged on his shirt, working the buttons open.

"Sounds great. You can take the side-by-side out." Tomorrow. Not tonight. Tonight was about flying and loving.

"Mhm. I have a little side by side for you." Fox pushed his shirt off and went after his fly.

"I want more than side by side. I want everything."

Fox paused and caught his gaze, looking right into him. "Then I think we should move to the bedroom."

"I'd love that. Let me get the fire banked. Bring the wine?"

Fox stood, picked up their glasses and waited for him in the doorway. "Love watching you move."

"Love you, full stop." And it felt so fucking good to say.

"We're just getting started. Come on. I have your wine." Fox turned and headed for the bedroom, glancing over his shoulder at him. "Come on, baby."

"Coming!" Or he sure as shit hoped so.

Fox handed him his glass of wine in the bedroom and must have heard his thoughts. "Naughty."

"Yes, sir. I want to be a grown-up with my man. I want to see if you can scream."

"Yeah? I want to see if you can beg." Fox winked at him and swallowed the rest of his wine in one sip.

"Ooh... I do like a challenge." He sipped his and stopped to toe off his boots. That would save them time.

"I think I can make it happen." Fox went for his belt again, undoing it with practiced ease. Fox lowered his fly and pushed his jeans low on his hips, then touched him with warm fingers through his briefs.

"Mmm... you make me need wicked things, darlin'. You make me want to holler."

"I understand. Deeply." Fox kissed him again, fingers pushing under his briefs, hot palms resting against his ass.

He opened up, just offering Fox everything he had. Fuck, he loved this gorgeous son of a bitch.

Fox explored with a hot tongue, claiming every bit of his

mouth. Fox was hard behind his fly and pressed roughly against Trent's unprotected cock as Fox held their hips close enough to make them both ache.

He groaned, his hips rolling, humping up against his lover, giving himself a little bit of zing.

Fox tugged and turned him, then leaned hard until he fell onto the bed. Fox's chest was flushed, eyes focused on Trent as he pulled Trent's jeans off and went back for his briefs.

He flexed his abs, showing off a little, letting Fox admire.

"Gorgeous. God, you make me feel... dizzy."

"Good. Everyone deserves that." To have someone that made them feel dizzy.

Fox kept staring as he undressed, adding his clothing piece by piece to the pile until he was wearing nothing but his fading summer tan.

Trent held his arms open for his lover, offering him a smile. "C'mere, darlin'. I got a need."

"Do you?" Fox climbed over him, seeming larger and stronger somehow when he was naked. Fox's voice was rough with need. "Tell me all about it."

He heard what Fox was asking. He got it. "I need you to fuck me, darlin'. Show me how much I make you ache."

"Such a mouth on you, cowboy." Fox reached for their lube and nodded to him. "I'll make it good for you, baby."

"I know." He didn't doubt it in the least. He trusted Fox with his whole soul. His body was easy.

Fox kissed him again and gently nudged his knees wider so he could settle between them. Fingers wrapped around his cock and stroked slowly, giving him a little more buzz. His man wasn't in any hurry.

All Trent could do was lick his lips, staring at Fox as his man touched him, petted him. Fuck him, that was hot.

The pop of the lube bottle was enough to make him tingle in anticipation, and a second later, cool fingers slid across his hole, teasing and tempting. "Just going to get you ready, nice and slick; you just relax."

"You won't hurt me." He knew it. Fox was his man. "And I need you, more than anything."

Fox let out a little moan. "You're making it so damn hard to be patient." He felt that sweet pressure as Fox pushed a finger inside him, testing, watching him.

"Mmhmm... I hear you, but you can do it. Be patient."

Fox's eyes flashed. "Oh, I can. I will be very patient. You're just so smoking hot right now you're not making it easy on me. That's not a bad thing, baby."

Trent loved to hear that—Fox made him feel ten-thousand feet tall and bulletproof. "I trust you."

Fox eased a second finger in, stretching him gently, twisting them and making him feel it. "I love you. You're going to feel so good."

He drew one foot up, exposing himself. His cock ached, so heavy and full.

Fox's third finger was tight and that stretch burned a little, setting his nerves on fire. "I trust you, too. With everything. All of me. Things I never let anyone else see."

"You honor me. To the bone." He cupped Fox's jaw, groaned deep in his chest.

Fox kissed him, hard and hungry, and replaced those fingers with a hot cock, nudging against him. Fox was gentle at first, teasing them both before pushing inside him slowly. "Oh, fuck."

"Love." His eyes felt huge, pulling at the corners. "I feel you everywhere."

Fox nodded, swallowing before he spoke. "Just you and me in the whole universe."

All Trent could do was breathe with Fox, feel. Fuck, he was high as a kite, aching for sensation.

Fox settled over him, rocking them steadily, looking into his eyes. "You feel so good."

"Hope so." His eyes crossed. "Don't fucking stop. Please."

"Not—not stopping." Fox grunted and rocked a little harder until their bodies were tight together.

Trent couldn't hold in his shivers, the moans that poured out through his body in waves.

Fox had gotten stronger working on the ranch, and the muscles in his shoulders and arms popped as he worked to keep his balance. They'd built a driving rhythm now, their sounds filling the darkening room.

"Harder. More, darlin'. Please." His entire body was on fire.

Fox heard him and shifted, thrusting harder, pushing that one knee up higher so he felt it deeper. "I... soon, baby. You with me?"

"Fuck yes. Right. Here." Words. Go him.

Fox nodded and let loose, hips pumping. His brow furrowed in a beautifully needy way, an expression Trent knew was one of those things his lover only shared with him.

He met every thrust, hips rolling to add his strength to Fox's. Fuck, he was so close.

"Trent—" Fox groaned and went still for a second, eyes closing to just slits. He felt that heavy cock swell inside him as Fox's orgasm seemed to take over the man's entire body— mouth gaping, arms trembling, and a beautiful blush spread across Fox's skin.

"Fuck..." It took two quick tugs to his prick, added to that hungry expression in Fox's eyes, to push Trent over the edge.

Fox moaned and rocked into him a little more, then kissed him hard, stealing what little breath he had in him.

It was like Fox had opened him up and put his happy ass back together.

Fox rolled and landed beside him with a soft groan, then those long arms reached out and pulled him close. "You're amazing. Beautiful."

The best—the absolute best—he could do was moan.

"Mhm." Fox held him, kissed his temple, and ran fingers through his hair. "I know, baby. I love you."

"Love you." He was floating, just swinging nice and easy. "Keeping you. Forever."

21

They'd found the cows, and they'd put the little pen where Amelia's minis lived back together, and moved them out of the garage.

Not bad for a morning's work, even if it felt way cooler out here than it had before.

Fox took a swig from the water bottle Trent had just given him and squinted at what was left of the barns.

It wasn't much.

"I need to learn to ride." He turned to Trent and grinned. "Horses, I mean."

"Sure. You want to start with the tiny ones?" Oh, that was mean.

Fox snorted and crossed his arms. "And to think I was so good to you last night."

"You were amazing last night. Amazing." Trent looked great in his long-sleeved T-shirt, strong and sure as he came over to steal a kiss.

The compliment made him feel taller, confident, things he'd had a hard time holding onto until recently. Things that seemed to come more naturally after last night. "Mmm.

Thank you. Things just keep getting better between us, don't they?"

He really thought so. It made things like losing a barn feel less like a disaster. They had everything. They could build a barn.

Trent beamed like he'd been lit up from within. "They do. And we're fixin' to have our holiday season—I can't wait to have a reason to decorate. I got my guy and my Ames."

"Are we having your family for Thanksgiving? Your sister, right? Your parents?"

"We'll all eat at Rope's. His kitchen's bigger, but yeah. We'll have a houseful."

"Wow. I'm not used to big holiday things with family and everything. I'm looking forward to it. Mostly." He gave Trent a wink. Trent understood he had to kind of ease into crowds these days. But he could do it. He wanted to learn about that surrounded-by-family feeling.

"Well, we have Thanksgiving, Friendsgiving, and Amelia says she's been invited to go shopping at the crack of dawn by Jennifer and her kids..."

Cash for Amelia, got it.

"That's a lot of celebrating. Is Christmas like that too?" He should have known, given the size of the Halloween crowd, that Rope and Jude's house was celebration central.

He grinned and rolled his eyes. "Oh, lord. I don't know about the school and stuff, but there are parties, and plays, and get-togethers for the whole damn season. We do love our holidays, and we'll ride in the Christmas parade in town."

"Ride, huh?" He leaned close to his man. "I don't think the minis will hold me for a whole parade."

"You can ride in the wagon with the kiddos if you want.

Be in charge of them with Jude." Trent rolled his eyes. "They stand up a lot."

"I am going to learn to ride, damn it." He snorted. "I am not Jude. You're going to make me a cowboy."

"You'll be doing that, all by yourself." Trent kissed his nose. "But we'll get you on a horse. No worries."

"Good. That's what I want. I want to ride. And I'm going to learn about building barns too." This was his home now, and he was going to be useful, learn, and know what he was talking about.

He was going to help Trent make this place a successful thing, and he was going to have a ball doing this and being a dad.

"Speaking of barns, do you have someone coming out soon? I'd love to talk with them when they get here."

Trent nodded, a curious expression flitting across his face. "I got the Johnsons coming out this afternoon. They do reasonable work, but it's quality."

"Cool. I can sit in on your talk with them?"

"Darlin', you're financing the barns. I reckon we're meeting them together."

Okay, that felt amazing. Not only that Trent accepted his help, but that his cowboy tucked him into the family, into the ranch.

"*We* are financing the barns, but yes, that would be great." Everything that was his was his family's now. "And I, uh. I have something for you." He pulled a business card out of his wallet and handed it to Trent. "That's the surrogate service I used for Amelia."

Trent's eyebrow went up, and his head tilted. "Yeah?"

"Mhm. I was thinking maybe you should give them a call." He winked at Trent, enjoying the curious look in Trent's eyes.

"I might think about that, but I have to tell you, Mr. Fox. I'm a traditional type of guy."

"All right, Mr. James." He smiled, knowing exactly what Trent meant, and it wasn't about having a baby the traditional way because that was impossible. "I was thinking champagne and candles and a crackling fire or something, but I don't need any of that. We can do this right here with the mini horses and the chickens."

He didn't have a ring, but he felt like the moment mattered more than the hardware. "You're already my family and Amelia's family. I seem to suddenly own yaks, and I'm all in on building a barn, so there's really only one thing left that I don't have. It's pretty important to me too so, Trent James," he said, going down on one knee. "Will you be my husband?"

He wasn't nervous or anxious at all until the words were out of his mouth. He was sure Trent was going to say yes, of course he was, but now that the question was out there, he worried that he should have waited. What if Trent would rather he had a ring? Maybe this wasn't romantic enough? The "what-ifs" were suddenly making his heart pound and all he could do was hope.

Please say yes.

Trent grinned at him, those warm eyes searching his before the grin turned into a huge, sunny smile. "There's nothing I want more, darlin'. Not a thing."

"Yes!" He popped right up, smiling so hard it hurt, and caught Trent in a tight hug. "I love you. Thank you."

"I love you." Trent held him close, humming deep in his chest. "I can't wait to tell Ames that you asked."

He felt a little studly if he was honest. Strong and tall, like he was Superman. And he loved that Trent wanted to be the one to break the news. "Me either."

"Kiss me again, darlin'. We got work to do."

"I can do that." Fox made just enough room between them for that kiss, and it was full of love and the future.

He and his fiancé were going to buy a barn.

Enjoyed Fox & Trent? Want a FREE bonus chapter?
Follow the link below!
https://readerlinks.com/l/4723317

WANT MORE BA & JODI?

Interested in learning more about our East Meets Westerns?

Join BA & Jodi's Newsletter
https://lp.constantcontactpages.com/sl/nzvRTTy

Patreon: https://www.patreon.com/BATortuga
There are lots of tiers to chose from, and also free serial stories.
Discord: https://discord.gg/Vba5P5Qv
BA's Discord server has a channel for BA/Jodi related chat and info.

Hey, Y'all!

We want to thank you for giving Outfoxed a try. We hope you enjoyed the story and want to check out the rest of the series.

If you can spare a few minutes to post a review at the retail website where you made your purchase, we'd very much appreciate it!

Yeehaw and thanks for reading!

BA & Jodi

ABOUT JODI

JODI takes herself way too seriously and has been known to randomly break out in song. Her queer MCs are imperfect but genuine, stubborn but likable, often kinky, and frequently their own worst enemies. They are characters you can't help but fall in love with while they stumble along the path to their happily ever after. For those looking to get on her good side, Jodi's obsessions include nonfat lattes, basketball (go Celtics!), and tequila any way you pour it.

Website: jodipayne.net

Newsletter: https://readerlinks.com/l/2317334

All Jodi's Social Links: linktr.ee/jodipayne

ABOUT BA

Western to the bone and an unrepentant Daddy's Girl, BA Tortuga spends her days with her hounds and her beloved wife, having mother-daughter dates, and eating Mexican food. When she's not doing that, she's writing. She spends her days off watching rodeo, knitting, and surfing Pinterest in the name of research. Following their own personal joys, BA and Julia heard the call of the high desert and they now live in the New Mexico mountains. BA's personal saviors include her wife, her best friends, and coffee. Lots of coffee. Really good coffee.

Having written everything from fist-fighting cowboys to rural single dads to werewolves, BA does her damnedest to tell the stories of her heart, which is committed to giving everyone their happily ever after. With books ranging from heart-warming stories of found families, to rodeo cowboys that are fighting to make a mark, to fiery passionate love affairs, BA refuses to be pigeon-holed by anyone but the voices in her head.

BA loves to talk to her readers and can be found at http://batortuga.com/ and her newsletter signup link is http://bit.ly/BAJulianews

AVAILABLE FROM JODI & BA

<u>East Meets Westerns</u>

The On the Ranch Series

Tending Tyler

Roped In

Diamonds in the Rough

Outfoxed

The Wrecked Universe

Wrecked

Flying Blind

Special Delivery, A Wrecked Holiday Novel

Seeds and Sunshine

Pickup Man

Cowboy for Sale

The Merry Everything Series

Window Dressing

Cowboy Protection

Cowboys and Cupcakes

Thawed Out

A Present for Parker

The Higher Elevation Series

Heart of a Cowboy

Keeping Promises

Bigger Than Us

Home Free

<u>**BDSM/Kink**</u>

The Cowboy and the Dom Trilogy

First Rodeo, Book One

Razor's Edge, Book Two

No Ghosts, Book Three

The Soldier and the Angel, a Cowboy and Dom Novel

The Sin Deep Series

(set in The Cowboy and the Dom Universe)

Sin Deep

Trouble with Cowboys

The Triskelion Series

Breaking the Rules

Making a Mark

Making the Rules

Les's Bar Series

Just Dex

Hide Bound

Wholly Trinity

New Tricks

Lost Boy

The Barn Series

Zeke & Wesley

Other Titles

The Collaborations Series

Refraction

Syncopation

Puzzles Series

Cryptic

Single Titles

Temptation Ranch

Land of Enchantment

Summit Springs Sapphic (F/F) Romance

Christmas Bizarre

Honeymoon in the Cards

www.ingramcontent.com/pod-product-compliance
Lightning Source LLC
Chambersburg PA
CBHW051052050726

47592CB00002B/491